Nathrotep

William H. Nelson

Blysster Press

ASHTON,
THANKS FOR YOUR
SUPPORT!
BEST WISHES!
William H Nel

Website: www.williamhnelsonbooks.com
Facebook: www.facebook.com/williamhnelsonbooks

"Nathrotep" Printing History
Blysster Press paperback edition March 2018

Blysster Press

A new kind of publisher for a new kind of world.

ISBN 978-1-940247-37-3

Printed in the United States of America
www.blysster.com

Dedicated, In Loving Memory,
To Theresa M. Nelson

Acknowledgments

First and foremost, I would like to thank Lisa Paschke. Without her encouragement and support, I wouldn't be the person that I am today, let alone an aspiring writer. If it wasn't for her, this book might never have seen the light of day. Also, I would like to thank Charity Becker for all her patience and in-depth instruction throughout the editing and revision process. Truly, without her help, this book would never have been published at all. In addition to these two people, I would also like to thank Tara Gilliam. She's the only person I know who you can call up at 3 in the morning and still get good feedback without too much grumpiness. Her suggestions, and in fact her encouragement that I write this book in the first place, has been invaluable. And a special thanks goes out to Kyle Penney for his support and the proofreading that he helped with right at the very start all those years ago. If there is anyone else that I missed, I apologize for leaving you out and promise that I'll try and remember to mention you in my next book! Thanks again to everyone for reading this and continuing to support me in my endeavors to write. It is very much appreciated.

Day One
Wednesday, April 27th, 1988
-1-

The smell of incense clung to her as she stood shivering in the dank air. This could not be happening, and yet it was. She was in a chamber buried deep beneath the earth, her surroundings wavering in the thin, uncertain light cast from infrequent candles. Paralyzed by a sense of pure terror, she stood transfixed as the shadows swelled around her and slid upward into the spaces above.

Tears blurring her eyes, she glanced about, the fear clutching greedily at her thundering heart. To either side were only waves of darkness, flickering and dancing, but before her was the sight which captured her unwilling attention. A low altar stone, painted by the feeble glow of the diminutive candles, sat nestled beneath a swirling chaos of rippling energy. It throbbed under the vortex like a living thing.

As its foul malignancy washed over her, she searched for breath enough to scream. Finding none, she slid to her knees in the acrid, clinging darkness, praying for release from the paralyzing emotions that held her fast. The robed figure was there, like always, his filthy, black cowl shrouding him in the colors of the grave. Waves of noxious evil poured from him like clouds boiling in the forefront of a terrible storm, and the hellish ritualistic dagger poised in his upflung fist seemed to pulse to the pounding of her frightened heart.

She cried out then, somehow becoming one with the blade as it struck down toward the small figure chained to the stone. The hatred, the blind rage, the mind-numbing, soul-shattering vileness coursed through her. She was the knife, the cascading energy within it, and the towering, all-consuming bleakness of evil inherent within the very room. And, as she struggled in vain, trying with frantic urgency to stop herself from the violent impressions, the blade that was her struck deep into the captive child's breast.

**

Robin awoke with a shrill scream. Stunned and panting, she lay in the dampness of her own sweat, the sheets rucked and knotted around her slender, adolescent body. For a moment, she couldn't tell where she was, the images of that hateful chamber still etched into her mind like patterns carved into living glass. The dream surrounded her. With maddened intensity, her eyes darted about the room, not really seeing the posters of George Michael, the small, color television, or the stuffed animals on the chair by the window. Her gaze spun wildly around, searching for the black priest, the living blade.

After what seemed like hours, her heart slowed its maddened pounding and her tear-streaked vision cleared enough to take in the normal, everyday clutter of her small living space. She recognized the vanity mirror with its many pictures of her and her friends, the dresser with its customary plethora of knickknacks, and the pile of unfolded laundry heaped by the closet door. Gulping in huge breaths of air, she fought to further calm herself. It was, after all, only a dream, wasn't it?

Or was it something more?

No, she told herself, shaking her head in a violent, twisting motion, it was only a dream. Another nightmare. Although she could still remember most of it: the dark, incense-filled chamber, the helpless child chained to the altar stone, and the figure of the vicious priest, raising the repellent dagger in his hate-filled grasp. The extreme vividness of it frightened her. Getting out of bed, she tried to rid her mind of the lingering images as she shuffled down the hallway and into the bathroom.

After shedding her sweat-soaked nightgown, she turned on the shower and stepped in. As the heated water poured over her, she felt her thoughts clearing, the visions of the dream receding to the back of her mind like fireflies fading with the dawn. Soon, after a vigorous scrubbing, she was refreshed and unhindered by the disturbing imagery, no longer even thinking on it as she toweled herself dry.

Standing before the mirror, she began to run a comb through her wavy brown hair, judging herself critically through narrowed hazel eyes. Not altogether unattractive, she decided, but also not exactly the prettiest girl at her school. As she dressed, her thoughts turned to Mark Cook. If only he'd notice her, see her as someone he'd want to spend more time with. No, she thought, a light blush creeping across her freckled cheeks, Mark had bigger fish to fry. It was no secret how he felt toward Kelly; all the boys felt that way. Suffering a momentary flash of jealousy for her best friend's good looks and easy grace, she finished tucking in her blouse and adjusted the belt that encircled her petite, denim-clad waist. As she rechecked her reflection once more for unseen blemishes, she heard her mother calling from the kitchen.

"Robin, you'll miss the bus if you don't hurry up!"

"I'll be there as soon as I dry my hair, Mom," she shouted. After whirling the blow dryer's hot breath through her hair, she threw a small can of hairspray and a selection of makeup into her purse, then hurried down the hall.

As she ran out the kitchen door, she waved to her mom. "Bye, Mom; see you tonight."

"What about breakfast?" her mother called, but Robin was already out of sight.

***

The street she lived on was a typical American suburb. All the houses were the same drab architecture that marked the degradation of craftsmanship that had come with rapid development and cheap building supplies. Most of the homes were the type that were thrown together almost overnight by greedy businessmen who'd bought out the area years ago seeking profit from the sale of affordable living. Some of it, however, predated the entire town.

At the end of the road was an old graveyard that dominated the landscape. It had become a landmark in the now thriving community having been there as far back as anyone could remember. The land that it crouched upon was sprawling and extensive, consisting of many acres of prime real estate. But the brooding, age-old monument was not for sale at any price. A great number of well-loved kinfolk had been laid to rest there over the years, and any attempt to purchase the property would have been met with the strongest of opposition. The land developers had wisely decided to build around the site, even using it to boost sagging property sales by claiming that the historical landmark added an air of 'quaint mystery' to the area.

As she headed toward the bus stop, Robin glanced up at the abandoned caretaker's house that perched atop the steep, overgrown incline, and was startled to see a flash of movement in one of the upper story windows.

"Hey!" she called out to her friend who stood waiting for her. "Someone's in the old house on Graveyard Hill!"

"Where?" Kelly asked, peering up at the house, "I don't

see anything. . ."

"There." Robin pointed, turning to squint back up at the dilapidated structure. "In the attic window. Hey! They disappeared!"

Laughing, her friend leaned on her, placing an arm around her shoulder. "You really had me there for a minute, Robin."

Kelly Miller, like many girls of her generation, had been forced to mature quickly, perhaps even too quickly. With her deep blue eyes, long golden hair, and winning smile, she was much sought after by the boys at her school. Robin knew, and actually Kelly had never made it much of a secret, that she just used the ones she liked and led the others on, taking great pleasure from their fruitless attentions. She had once told Robin she never had to worry about any pain that might arise from an uncertain relationship that way, but Robin knew it was just a flimsy excuse; Kelly had been hurt early on by a boy who'd played her in much the same way. It was a vicious cycle, but it kept her from the mindless depression she'd suffered in the aftermath of the previous romance. Now she was smirking at Robin, her head tilted to one side in mock solicitude.

"There was someone there! I really saw them!" Robin insisted.

"Come on now, you don't expect me to fall for that crap, do you?"

"There was someone in that window. I'm telling you the truth!"

"Alright, alright! You saw someone in the old caretaker's house. So what? I wasn't calling you a liar. Really, Robin, you take everything too seriously." Turning, she glanced down the street. "Here comes the bus. . ."

"I'm sorry," Robin blurted, the disturbing images surging back to the forefront of her mind, "it's just these nightmares I'm having—they seem so real! I'm almost afraid to sleep."

As the bus pulled up to the curb, Kelly turned and considered the rambling old structure. Turning back, she smiled again, a mischievous glint in her eyes.

"Are you coming to my slumber party this weekend?" she inquired.

"I think so; I still have to ask my mom, but I'm pretty sure I can go."

"That's great!" Kelly said, taking her arm. Within seconds, the conversation had turned to the other girls who'd be at the party, the inevitable phone calls they'd make, and all the things they planned to do on the upcoming Saturday evening.

Entering the vehicle, they walked to the back and took a seat, still talking about their big plans. As the bus began to move forward once more, creeping off down Mercury Street, there was no one left to hear the chilling, deranged laughter reverberating from deep within the house on top of Graveyard Hill.

-2-

Carol LePrade sometimes had to work long hours at the hospital, but the pay was good, and being a nurse was something that she really enjoyed. In her heart, she felt that she was giving a lot back to the community, especially after all she'd taken from it. But it did her no good to dwell on the past; it was done and over with and she had made a new life for herself. Still, the choices she'd made had been quite difficult.

This morning she had hoped to spend some time with her daughter, but now she was shaking her head in annoyance as she put away the breakfast dishes. Ever since the loss of her husband eleven years ago, she'd struggled to raise her daughter on her own. She liked to think she'd been somewhat successful, but at times she seriously doubted her ability. Robin was headstrong, rebellious to a fault, and sometimes infuriating. On the other hand, she was intelligent, spontaneous, and what many would refer to as happy-go-lucky.

Carol was not at all sure that these were entirely good qualities.

Sighing, she began to clean the countertops and furnishings that occupied their small kitchen and dining room. Humming a bit to herself, she let her thoughts wander as she stared out the window. She was polishing the surface of a teakwood cabinet when she accidentally bumped against a picture frame, sending it tumbling to the floor. Leaning forward, she reached down to pick it up.

Seeing the image inside the old frame, she faltered, running her hand over the picture while trying to repress her swelling emotions. The somber face of her late husband stared out at her, his right hand resting on her shoulder as his left arm enfolded their giggling daughter. His eyes penetrated deep into her soul and she was unable to look away, tears running freely down her cheeks. The past was done, but some things would never truly go away. She stood that way, wrapped in painful memories, for quite some time.

***

After an uneventful day at school and a mediocre dance recital, Robin had been more than happy to head home for the evening. She'd had little enough sleep the night before and it was starting to catch up to her. After eating a late dinner of leftover Chinese food, she put her dishes in the sink and started toward her room at the opposite end of the house.

Her mother had been rather distant tonight. Sure, she was sometimes a bit melancholy, but tonight she'd appeared to be filled with a strange emptiness and an almost total lack of awareness. She sat in an old, overstuffed chair in the corner of the living room, pulling at a strand of her curling, auburn hair while staring off into the distance. Robin knew about her mother's sudden mood swings, but this seemed different. Maybe there was something wrong? No, the bleakness would pass as it always did, given enough time. Confident that things would work themselves out, she smiled at her in a reassuring way.

"I'm totally beat; I guess I'll do my homework and go to bed. I'll see you tomorrow, Mom. . . I love you."

Her mother gave her a distracted nod and a faint smile in return as she passed through the living room and headed off down the hallway.

After finishing up her book report, Robin crawled into bed and fell into a slumber that was deeper than it had ever been. The mists rose up and swirled around her, dragging her through the doors of night and into the dread world that lay beyond.

The chamber was nebulous, the candles spaced widely apart in the shadowy depths. To the right and left of her, shrouds of darkness licked and devoured the feeble light. Swaying, Robin's attention was yet again drawn toward the altar stone. It was there that the answers were to be found. In that obscure cavern, sealed away by the forces of shadow, the brutal scene replayed itself over and over in the depths of her slumbering mind.

The priest was there, as always, the wicked dagger grasped in his upflung fist. But this time she could almost make out his features in the dim illumination. The cold, grasping darkness surrounded her, stifling her whimpers with an onrushing tide of evil malignancy, but she was somehow able to retain a semblance of control.

There was something different this time, something extraordinary, that she could sense deep within herself. She felt compelled to try and stop the evil figure clad in the soot black robes. In fact, this time she would stop him!

Edging forward, her teeth chattering and legs wobbling, she fought her way to a small candelabrum just to the left of the altar. Stumbling up against it, she grabbed it in a clumsy, two-fisted grip. Then, she swung it around.

The priest turned at the last minute, somehow alerted to the threat, but he was too late to avoid it; the blaze ignited him as the sputtering candles grazed against his fetid robes. Consumed by the flames, his body became a paroxysm of smoking fire. Flailing in agony, fiery arms brushed aside the robe's hood, exposing twin orbs of smoldering fury where his eyes had once been. A gasping shriek erupted from him as the flesh melted from his skull in bloody rivulets like the flowing of hot, meat-colored wax.

Sitting bolt upright in bed, Robin found she was on the verge of hysteria. It was a dream, she told herself, not really believing it, only a dream. She tried to throw off the covers, but couldn't seem to get her arms to function. Sweat poured off her in the darkness, making the room even more unpleasant as she twisted, gasping, onto her side.

A dream, only a dream.

Or was it?

Then, she heard a faint noise coming from her bedroom window. A kind of soft scratching sound that sent fresh chills crawling up and down her spine. Drawing on all her courage, she stilled her quaking body, then turned her head, bit by bit, toward the window.

Uncontrolled spasms overcame her as her blood ran cold.

Just outside the window stood a ghastly apparition of both horror and repulsiveness. Huge, luminescent eyes glared at her as rotted lips curled back in a gruesome sneer, exposing jagged, yellow teeth. Pieces of decayed flesh and moldering vegetation hung from its face and body and, as she watched in growing horror, a greenish-brown slime oozed from its almost nonexistent nose. Its bony claw scratched lightly on the window pane as it spoke to her in a hellish, rasping voice.

"Let me in, Robin. . . let me in. . ."

Then it laughed. Not an amused or happy sort of sound, but a snarling chortle that sent pieces of flesh and strands of spittle flinging from its blackened tongue.

Quivering in total mind-numbing terror, she found her voice and screamed. The shriek rebounded off her poster-strewn walls and cascaded in and out of the corners like an agile wraith, causing her to wail even louder with the unexpected volume of it.

Regaining her strength of will, she leapt from the bed and darted down the hall, jerking open her mother's bedroom door. She was unprepared for what she saw.

Her mother lay in a pool of dark, congealing blood, the curtains mocking her from where they rustled to either side of the shattered casement. Taking an involuntary step forward, she gazed down upon her mother's tortured face. The flesh had been peeled back to expose bloody strands of contorted muscle. Black holes, weeping sluggish, oily fluids, now marked where the clear blue eyes had once been.

Robin's body twitched violently as the chill night wind gusted across her from the gaping maw of the violated window. Outside, she could hear the creature moving and chuckling, running its bony fingers along the aluminum siding with an almost playful gentleness. Blood continued to drip from the bed, collecting on the floor with a metronomic popping sound that echoed strangely in the relative silence. Now she could smell the rotting thing through the miasma of blood and death, could hear it just outside the window.

It was coming in.

Turning toward it, she lost the ability to move as her entire body went rigid in shock. With a low, animalistic growl, it clambered over the sill and shambled toward her, its rotted clothing barely covering its emaciated figure. Glancing down from its leering expression, she began to detect other movements upon it—the movements of fat, grayish maggots and shiny beetles crawling over its putrid, exposed entrails. Reaching out, its bloody talons grasped and clutched for her as it sidled closer.

"I have come for you," it purred in its repellent voice. "You must let me in! Let me in, Robin. . ."

With that, it brayed out another laugh, spraying her with blood and sticky debris as its fetid breath washed over her. She tried to back away but her legs refused to work, and she knew then that there could be no escape. Its bony claws snaked around her to clutch at her back, descending, kneading, pinching, and circling down to firmly grasp at her buttocks. Drawing her close, it leaned its unwholesome face down to hers as if for a long, repugnant kiss. . .

She awoke screaming. Her mother was there, holding her, saying, "It's all right, honey; it was a dream. . . only a dream. . ."

But her mouth still burned with the memory of its vile lips.

"Oh, Mom!" she sobbed, trembling against her. "It was so. . . so real!"

Her mother held her close for the rest of the night, coaxing her back to stability with a gentle touch and a consoling voice. During that time, not once did she notice the strangeness in her mother's eyes, nor the way she kept glancing toward the bedroom window.

Day Two
Thursday, April 28th, 1988
-3-

Power seemed to swell around him in the dusty air of the house as he moved upward from the places beneath. The stairs were rickety and the railings had long since rotted away, but he didn't notice the decrepitude around him. He was in a fine mood. Trailing a gnarled, dirt-encrusted hand along the gray, flaking wall, he chuckled as he made his way toward the attic above.

Zacheriah Tate, or 'Zak', as his friends had once called him, was quite mad. Not the type of everyday insanity that many people suffer from, but an all-consuming twisting of the mind and body that he was quite aware of. In fact, he was grateful for it—it deadened the pain he carried, turning it from a vortex of inner emotional turmoil to a harmless background throbbing that did little more than annoy him.

He smiled, a twitch of thin lips pressed tightly together under his filthy, brownish-gray beard. Yes, the pain was always there, and he had carried it for a long time. The dangerous amounts of alcohol and illicit drugs he had taken over the years had helped some, but even they could not completely kill the memories or return the happiness he once had known. That would change, he knew, and soon; his new friends had promised him that. He smiled again, a low moan escaping his lips as he once more traveled the familiar pathways of haunting memory.

He no longer tried to repress the memories as he once had done. It never worked; the thoughts would always betray him, conveying him into the past to repeatedly add to his torment. He would never forget, could never forget.

He'd been eighteen at the time, working for Grizzly Advertising. They were a small, Seattle-based shop, but he'd been quickly rising in popularity within the company. Working as a freelance artist had seemed like a dream. The hours made themselves and he was doing something he was extremely good at. The workload steadily increased as clients started asking for him by name, and his preoccupation had let him concentrate on something besides his heartfelt loneliness. He not only lacked many of the qualities that women found attractive, but he was also painfully shy at the time. He was what some would call a 'late bloomer'. His experience with relationships had consisted of several broken dates and much outright disdain.

He was not a lucky guy.

Then, that had all changed. His uncle died, leaving him with a small personal fortune consisting of several thousand dollars. Women began to take notice, and one in particular. It was Barbara Sanders, a girl who worked part-time in the same building. She was beautiful; a stunning blonde with ice blue eyes and a devastating body. For the better part of three months, he'd been trying to get her to notice him. Not in any overt way, but in subtle, shy little hints and innuendos. None of that had worked, of course, until he'd received his inheritance. That's when she decided to take an interest.

Imagine his surprise when she called him out of the blue one Friday afternoon, crying and asking to come over to 'talk'. Of course, he'd readily accepted; they had spoken fleetingly enough for him to know that her current boyfriend was no prince. She was always saying what an insensitive jerk he was. So, hanging up the phone in a state of happy bewilderment, he had gone to meet her and bring her back to his small, out of the way apartment.

Their talk was enlightening, to say the least. She had broken it off with her current lover, and by the end of the evening, he had received the first kiss of many in their soon to become whirlwind relationship.

Snarling at the memory, he reached the top of the stairs. Turning, he headed down a large hallway, kicking piles of rotted cloth and old broken down cardboard boxes out of the way. Sinking back again into his musings, he assaulted the next stairwell leading upward.

Oh, yes! She had really wound him around her little finger. In two short weeks, she'd turned him from a shy introvert into a thriving sexual animal and outgoing socialite. In the space of the following months, they had acted out every fantasy that he'd ever envisioned and he had made many friends in the popular, drug-imbibing crowds.

He paid for everything, of course. The food, the wine, the copious amounts of coke, marijuana, LSD, and whatever else they could get their hands on. Also, he paid the rent, the car insurance, and all the bills.

It was the single most electrifying year in his life. He could not have cared less that the money was dwindling, and that they'd both lost their jobs due to an accumulation of absences. It did not matter to him that he no longer even looked at his art supplies. He was, for the first time in his life, deeply in love and beyond happy. The world was a great place to be, and he lived on the edge, every moment a new adventure, every precious second in her arms, an explosion of ecstasy. And he thrived on it.

Then, the money ran out.

He was forced into one dead-end job after another, trying hard to make ends meet and still keep up with their rapidly moving lifestyle. She, of course, did nothing in the way of work; it was no longer something she cared to do. Then, one day, he came home to an empty flat. She had finally snuck away, off to find bigger and more lucrative game.

His life was shattered. Bleakness and despair descended on him like a shroud, cloaking him in misery that would be with him for the rest of his life. Here was the root of his pain, the event that started him over the edge. His friends had tried to help, bringing him drugs and alcohol to blunt the icy stabs of loneliness that forever besieged him. Nothing worked. Even his parents knew something was wrong and tried to find him help, but it was a losing battle. Finally, in desperation, he borrowed some cash and decided to follow her.

He had a pretty good idea of where she'd gone, and he was right. She'd washed up in a little hole-in-the-wall town near Arizona called Plentsville. Her parents lived there, and it was only a matter of time before she went looking for a free handout.

Reaching the second-story landing, he chuckled to himself. Oh, yes! Good old Plentsville! The very town that he was now visiting again over ten years later. They had never caught him, and they never would. His new friends had assured him of that!

Yes, he had followed her here, all those years ago. It had taken him almost six months to find her, and he was about out of money by the time he did. She was staying with an older man in a house not too far from the graveyard. When he'd finally pinpointed her exact location, he'd waited patiently for the opportunity to confront her.

Finally, he got his chance.

The older man—he never did find out his name—always went out at the same time each day, leaving Barbara all alone. So, he waited until the man had left, and then entered the house from the garage. He found her in the bedroom, curled up in front of the T.V.

It was good to see her again, he remembered, the effects of the last ten hits of acid he'd taken just kicking in as he confronted her. She was surprised to see him, yet unafraid. When he demanded an explanation, she had scornfully showed him her belly. At first, he didn't comprehend, the colors and angles of the room swelling and contorting within his drug-filled mind, but then it hit him:

She was pregnant.

As he stood in shocked amazement, she began taunting him. She started by telling him that it was his child she carried but he would never see it, then went on to say that he might as well slink back to his nonexistent life and leave 'them' alone. After that, she'd reached for the phone, and that was her final mistake.

Something snapped in him that day. The pain, the loss, the fear, all of it mixed within him, seething through his drug-befuddled frame with torturous paroxysms of pure and unbridled rage. It was an agony so exquisite that he began to gibber and laugh as it took hold of him, a puppet tensing on the strings of his inner turmoil.

He could no longer contain it.

The phone cord he used to tie her to the bed. She was screaming, so he slammed a footstool up the side of her lovely face. She never knew what hit her. The stool shattered as he repeatedly slammed it against the wall above her unconscious body, screaming out her name over and over again. Then, grasping the splintered, jagged leg of the stool, madness raging through him, whirling in and out of his blurred vision like living cellophane paper, he'd torn open her womb, wresting the child from her body with eager hands. Awakening, she had let out a gasping cry, her clear, blue eyes swiftly clouding over in agonizing pain. Then, stroking the fetus and chuckling, he'd held it out, showing it to her as only a proud father would. As the last, feeble light was dimming from her eyes, he had taken his son and fled.

Now, as he climbed the last flight of steps in the deserted house, he thought about the years he'd spent since then. They were a blur, a living hell that he himself had imposed upon his tortured soul. He had wandered aimlessly from town to town, stealing when he could, always drinking himself into a stupor when the booze was there, and living the life of a vagrant that was really no life at all.

He had never stopped loving her, could never stop. As the years went by and he learned to suppress the pain, he slowly crossed the gap from one of the living to one of the walking damned. Somehow, all these years later, he had found himself drawn back to this little piss-hole of a town, the town that had never succeeded in capturing him. It was more than just that, however; now he had a purpose.

Something had led him back to Plentsville, something stronger than life itself, and he was a part of it. He laughed again as he thought of what his new life would bring. They had promised him that, promised him a great many things! But he knew his new friends wouldn't let him down. Hadn't they given him back some of his lost happiness already?

A soft scrabbling sound came to him from behind the walls, pacing him as he made his way toward the attic, and he smiled.

Opening the door, he was just in time to see something crawling from a hole near the baseboards. It was thin and brown, like an old, crinkly, paper sack, its small, rodent-like claws scratching at the floorboards as it came scuttling toward him. He saw that a dead rat hung from its festering mouth, and it was chewing noisily as it advanced on him across the shadowy, paper-strewn floor.

"My son!" Zak exclaimed joyfully, opening his arms to the putrid thing.

-4-

Dr. Barnaby Williams had always considered himself a competent man, but running a small counseling office in Plentsville often gave him challenges that were not so easy to resolve. Although his results tended to be successful, his next patient presented him with somewhat of a conundrum. The more he delved into her particular case, the fewer answers he seemed to find. Now he sat twirling a pen through his fingers, scowling down at the file laid open on his desk.

Noticing the agitated motion of his hand, he stopped the pen's rotation and placed it on the desk with a small grimace. This was one client that he hadn't been able to fathom. She seemed in perfect health, was well liked at her work, and looked to have a bright future ahead of her. He picked up the folder, turning it over and tapping the spine of it against the palm of his other hand.

There was a certain bleakness about this patient he just didn't understand. However, she was still fairly new to him, and perhaps in a few more sessions she would feel comfortable enough to talk about what was really bothering her. Until then, he'd just have to focus on what little she did offer and hope to gain some insight into the cause of her actual distress. Sighing, he reached over and pushed the intercom button on the phone system.

"Terry, would you send in Ms. LePrade, please?"

"Dr. Williams," replied the warm, professional voice, "we have a special visitor today. I'll bring them right in."

Williams was grateful for his secretary's cleverness. Terry Bradford was a bright, young woman who'd become invaluable to him over the last few months. She was studying at the nearby university with courses that included psychology and other related topics. Now, in her own fashion, she'd let him know to expect more than one person, thereby keeping him from the awkwardness of surprise. It gave him a sense of calm satisfaction as he prepared to receive his next client and her somewhat mysterious guest.

***

The first thing Robin noticed on entering the doctor's office was the extensive collection of books. They lined the walls in rows of thick, hardbound volumes, some of them appearing quite old. The receptionist handed a clipboard with her new paperwork to the man behind the desk and then gave her a reassuring wink as she left. The man smiled warmly as he got up to shake her mother's hand.

"Good afternoon, Ms. LePrade. Who's our young visitor?"

"This is my daughter, Robin," her mother said, motioning her forward. "I've brought her in because she's been having some terrible nightmares. They've lasted for over a week now, and I was wondering if you might be able to help?"

He peered at her through rounded glasses, his expression, combined with his neatly trimmed facial hair, reminding her vaguely of an owl.

"Hmm, well, I'll certainly give it a try. Why don't you wait in the reception area and I'll call you in when we're through, okay? Please, make yourself comfortable, Robin, and I'll try to evaluate the cause of these dreams as best I can."

She sat down in a comfortable black leather chair, shifting around a little as her pulse fluttered and her hands became clammy with sweat. Once her mother left, the doctor looked at her with genuine concern. Mom may have a few minor problems, she thought, but it looks like she's getting decent help. These people seemed so professional, there was really no reason for her to be nervous.

So far, anyway.

Meanwhile, the doctor had resumed his seat, where he leaned back, fiddling with a pen. When he realized what he was doing, he set the pen down, and then came straight to the point.

"So, what sort of dreams have you been having, Robin?"

Easing back in the chair, she tried to relax as she began to tell the doctor about the nightmares. He took notes on the clipboard, asking her to go into more detail on several occasions. When they were through, she asked him what he thought was causing them.

"Well," he said, "most bad dreams are caused by anxiety or stress, or even an unresolved problem within the subject. Sometimes, nightmares can even be caused by trauma—"

"But, doctor," she cut in, "I don't have any problems. Well, not any serious ones, anyway. . ." Heat crept across her cheeks as she shifted her gaze to the floor, then marshaled enough courage to glance back up at him.

His regard was so compassionate that it made her feel somewhat foolish. What bothered her was of a personal nature and she'd hoped that she wouldn't have to go into it. Well, he was a doctor, and she was here to get help. Straightening her shoulders, she met his eyes with a boldness that she didn't quite feel.

"There's this boy I like," she began, "but he doesn't seem to notice me and I think he likes my best friend instead.

I guess I get a little jealous of her sometimes. But, that wouldn't make me have all these nightmares, would it?"

"Robin," he said gently, "these feelings are quite normal. You have nothing to be ashamed of. The dreams you're experiencing are far too vivid to be caused by your attraction to a suitable boy your own age."

"Well," she ventured, regaining her composure, "if not that, then what?"

"There are several reasons for this phenomenon," he began, leaning back in his chair, "I've had patients with repressed rage who've experienced similar visions, the terrifying images boiling up from unreleased, pent-up emotions. Another reason could be abuse, and I don't say that lightly, believe me. If there's anything you'd like to tell me, understand it will be kept in the strictest of confidence. I'm only here to help you, Robin, but, in order to do so, you must tell me everything about yourself. Can you do that?"

"But I've never been abused! And my mom and I always talk out our problems. I admit, sometimes we do fight —who doesn't? But she's never beaten me or anything."

"What about your father?" he asked, adding a notation to her file. "I know he's not with you anymore, but what do you remember about him?"

"Actually, I don't remember him at all. He's. . . he's just always been gone. The only memories I have are the pictures he left behind. . ."

"But, surely you remember something?" he pressed, setting aside the clipboard. "Your mother tells me he passed away when you were about five years old. Even I can remember things from when I was five. I know it must be painful, but please try; it could be very important to solving your problem."

"I'm sorry, doctor, but I really don't remember him." Shaking her head, she ran a slim hand back through her hair. "I'd tell you if I did, but I can't recall a thing about him. In fact, I can remember when I was six. My mother and I used to play dress-up together. She had this marvelous trunk of old clothes. You know, all sorts of outdated hats, robes, dresses and things. I remember how much fun it was to walk around in front of the mirror with all those big people's clothes on. We even had little tea parties with imaginary friends and everything. That's one of the earliest memories I have."

They began to talk about her past, her social life, even her friendships. Williams was trying hard to find some clue as to the cause of the nightmares by letting her talk through her memories, hopes, and feelings, but he was coming up empty-handed. There just wasn't anything there to justify the horrendous images she had described. It was beginning to frustrate him.

The only thing he could conclude was that there could be some kind of mental block associated with the lack of memories from her earliest years. Maybe there was a connection, but he was getting nowhere with conventional methods. He was, however, starting to understand and to like this young woman, and he wanted to help her in any way that he could. Drugs were out; he didn't think her condition warranted such drastic measures. And he was also hesitant to send her to another of his colleagues. He would have to try something himself.

"Robin," he said after he had learned all he could from their conversation, "I would like you to consider hypnosis. Now, I know that sounds a little phony, and maybe a bit scary, but it's really quite simple, and it would help me to understand these blank spots in your memory."

"But that doesn't make any sense!" Robin exclaimed, sitting forward in the chair. "How can you help me with hypnosis? I saw a guy on cable television make another guy act like a chicken once. I don't want to be a chicken. . ."

"Calm down, Robin," he replied, getting to his feet and

coming around the desk to sit next to her and take her hand. "I won't make you do anything silly or plant suggestions in your head to make you feel like a barnyard animal. I just want to take you back a little way into your past and try to find out what your childhood was like. I am fully qualified, and I'm bound by my Hippocratic oath not to pry into your private thoughts."

"Hypnosis? Are you sure that this is the only way? Isn't there something else you could do?"

"Well, there are other things we could try," he said, leaning back and pushing his glasses higher up on his nose. "I could prescribe medication that would help you sleep more soundly, which I hesitate to do in your case. It could do more harm than good, and it's not the best method for facing this problem. Or, I could put you into a sleep study, which I'm sure would be uncomfortable for you and your mother; any visit to a hospital can rack up a serious bill. However, I think this will be a much easier way to rid you of these dreams. I'll simply take you back in time to see what lies in your earlier childhood, then, after discerning the cause of your nightmares, I'll plant a suggestion in your mind that will help block them until we can work through it. It's really quite simple."

"Don't we need my mom's permission for something like that?" she asked, arching an eyebrow.

"This is a simple procedure," he reasserted with calm certainty. "I've done it many times with other patients in similar situations. There's no risk involved at all. You're over the age of consent, so I can assure you that we won't need your mother's permission in this particular case. And the worst thing you could expect to happen would be dizziness or a mild headache afterward. I'll be very careful that we don't cause you any more anxiety or additional stress. It's really quite safe."

"Well. . . okay," she managed, "if you're sure it will

work. . ."

Reaching into his pocket, he dug around for a moment, and then pulled out a large, valuable-looking pocket watch. "Nice, isn't it," he asked, holding it out to her with a smile. "It was given to me by my grandfather. Look inside."

She opened the front panel. It was made of silver and the face had Roman numerals instead of conventional numbers. There was even a small, ivory cross set in the back of the polished metal cover. The engraving read, 'Go with God, my Grandson' and was signed in a flowery script—Donald E. Williams. Closing it, she handed it back, dangling it from the thick, golden chain.

"It's beautiful," she breathed, unable to take her eyes off it.

He began to swing it in front of her, talking in a light, comforting tone. She leaned back in the chair, already beginning to feel more relaxed.

Williams noticed this and continued his soft dialogue.

"Your mind is at rest. . . as you follow the watch, you are traveling toward contentment. . . keep your eyes on the watch. . . you can feel yourself floating. . . your eyes are feeling heavier and want to close. . . let your body sink down as your muscles relax. . . breathe deeply, now. . . that's right. . ."

Soon, her eyes fluttered closed, and she was completely under. He leaned forward.

"Robin, can you hear me?"

"Yes. . ." came the whispered response.

"Good. Now, we're going to go back, back to when you were five. Remember the watch, Robin? Can you see the hands of the watch?"

"Yes. . ."

"Good. The hands are moving backward and time is moving back as well. The hands are spinning faster and faster each minute, and, as they move backward, so do the years of your life. You are taken back to when you were five. Are you with me, Robin? You are five years old. . ."

But Robin was already twisting about in the chair, moaning and whimpering like a small child. As he bent over her in growing concern, her body went into convulsions, the muscles jumping and twitching while spittle flew from her lips. Williams tried to talk her down, assuring her again and again that she was all right, that he was there with her and that she was safe, but it had no effect. She gibbered and thrashed, lashing out at his unprotected face as he moved to keep her from hurting herself. Then, her eyes snapped open and he lost all control of his voice; the eyes were solid, startling red, and completely lacking pupils.

"Robin?" he managed to whisper.

Jerking up off the chair, her distorted face split into a wicked grin as a harsh, guttural language erupted from her quivering lips.

"P'eran, ocktol'lo fiat! Aiieea! Aiieea! Nathrotep! Encudus, ick too dot unum sancredo'ro! Nathrotep. . . Nathrotep! She will be ours!"

Her arms moved through sinuous contortions as her small body lurched forward, backing him into a corner. Surveying the room, her now crimson-colored eyes passed over the desk, bookshelves, and other items, to come to rest upon the doctor. A low, throaty hiss issued forth from her sneering mouth.

Cowering away from that evil stare, he frantically searched his mind for some way to save himself. As she staggered closer, her features contorted with animalistic savagery, he threw up his arms in an instinctive effort to protect himself. The watch, still clutched in his trembling fingers, snapped open, and the thing that now inhabited Robin let out a low sibilation of purest hatred.

As this horrid sound washed over him, he was knocked back into the bookshelves by a sudden, concussive force.

Close to losing the last shred of his sanity, his mind spun in circles, his remaining thoughts scampering away like so many frightened rabbits. Still holding the watch out in front of him, he smelled ozone, felt his hand go numb, and then explode with a searing pain. Dropping the timepiece with an involuntary cry, he collapsed to the floor, clutching at his wrist and partially swooning in agony. For a few brief moments, the world grew dim, and he was lost to the darkness.

-5-

As quickly as it had begun, it was over. As he shook the cobwebs from his mind, he forced his eyes to refocus on Robin, his breath coming in short, sobbing gasps. She was laying halfway off the chair, her face as innocent and serene as it'd been but moments before. He drew in a deep, steadying breath, gathering his intellect, then wrestled himself back into control by sheer force of will. It was not easy. As he regained his composure, he realized that the girl's mother must never know what had happened here, and reminded himself, with no small amount of relief, that the office had been soundproofed for patient confidentiality.

It took him only moments to decide what needed to be done.

Moving to the chair, he resettled Robin, wiped the spittle from her chin, and arranged her limp body into a more comfortable position. Then, he hastened to straighten up the more obvious things that had been knocked about. He was just finishing when she regained consciousness.

"W-what happened? I feel so strange. . ."

Williams could only stare at her in disbelief.

"What's wrong? You look pretty upset. . ."

"What?. . . Oh! Nothing. Nothing at all," he said, pulling his thoughts back into order. "I guess we'll have to go with those sleeping pills after all, just until we have a better understanding of these. . . these dreams of yours. . . "

She peered at him in shocked amazement; he looked like hell and he was contradicting himself. What could have happened while she was hypnotized? Actually, it didn't really feel like she'd been hypnotized. Maybe he hadn't been able to put her under to begin with, and she said as much.

He looked at her with haunted eyes, then agreed. He had not been able to put her into a receptive, hypnotic state after all.

"Send your mother in, please," he finished in a hollow voice. "I'll discuss this further with her and prescribe a mild sedative. That should do the trick, I think. Yes, that will do quite nicely."

She was puzzled, but hoped she would get the chance to talk to him again. It felt good to get a few things off her chest, and he'd treated her more like an equal instead of some young kid. She only wished she could figure out why he'd been so different there at the end. Maybe he was upset about not being able to hypnotize her. Shrugging, she left the room.

As the door swung closed, Williams sagged back against the desk. He was grateful she hadn't noticed the faint, acrid odor hanging in the air. Glancing down, his eyes fixated on a smoldering object on the ground. His self-control wavered as he looked from the large burn on his hand to the lump of melted slag that had once been his ivory inlaid watch. As Robin's mother entered the room, he kicked it under the desk. It left a small burnt patch on the polished mahogany floor.

"You seem a bit shaken, doctor," Ms. LePrade observed, her voice high with suppressed emotion. "Can you tell me what's the matter with my daughter?"

"Nothing. . . nothing at all. . ." he replied succinctly. "Just a familiar case of, um. . . adolescent bad dreams. It's quite normal, really. I'll prescribe a sedative. Nothing strong, you understand, just a little something to help her sleep."

Returning to his desk, he bent down and scribbled out the prescription. "If these nightmares persist, have her take two of these. And, Ms. LePrade—watch her. Watch her closely."

Carol searched his haggard features as she took the small slip of paper. Nodding to herself as if she'd reached some kind of inner conclusion, she turned and stalked out of the office. He didn't even notice; as the door closed behind her, Dr. Barnaby Williams fell to his knees, grabbed the small, plastic trash can, and was very, very ill.

***

"Hello?"

"Robin, why weren't you in school today?"

It was Kelly. At least, Robin thought it was Kelly; the pills were stronger than she'd anticipated and the room seemed to be spinning out of focus. She knew she couldn't keep her eyes open for very much longer, so she struggled to tell her friend about her visit to the doctor. The details were a bit fuzzy, due to the effects of the drug, but Kelly seemed to understand.

"Well, you get some rest and I'll see you tomorrow. Be sure to ask your mom about the slumber party; it's gonna be great! I've got something special planned. Don't forget. See ya!"

As Kelly hung up, Robin began her descent into unconsciousness. As she drifted toward sleep, she could feel the tendrils of the nightmare reaching out to ensnare her. For a few brief moments, she struggled against it. Then the pills enfolded her in their dark embrace, and she knew no more.

***

Zak was furious. The entire night was a complete waste! Cursing, he rose from the center of the diagram.

Above him, spread out in unnatural clarity, the pathways lay open, shimmering and pulsing as he vented his rage to the heavens. The roof of the ancient dwelling no longer impeded his sight; his new friends had shown him the way, taught him the words. Now, however, the words weren't working.

Reaching down, he snatched up the worm-eaten tome from the floor, careful not to lose his place. Within the moldering old book he had found the ancient rituals of power and, for the past several nights, they had made it possible for him to do what was needed. Now, she seemed to be resisting all his efforts!

Snarling, he refocused on the entities inhabiting the realms beyond. They answered in their own guttural tongues, snaring his chaotic thought patterns and drawing him upward once more, teaching him, showing him the passages of the stars, pulling him through the wanderings of his own dementia, and placing him again onto the pathways of towering darkness. Once more, he sent tendrils of ancient energy out toward the child, but she was. . . inaccessible. He begged and pleaded, tempting and cajoling them, but the creatures refused to lend him any more of their inexhaustible strength. Bellowing out in frustration, he scratched long gouges of flesh from his already battered visage, raging from within the confines of the intricately drawn pattern.

As his anger spent itself, he slumped to the floor in defeat, letting the portal close; the child had resisted him a final time. Even with all the power he'd gained from the Kitab al Azif he was still unable to reach her. Up until now, the document had been his key, his gateway into the depths of her slumbering mind. Now, he realized he would need more than just the feeble materials he'd been using—more blood, more power. Yes, he would need much more! It had all been going so well, yet now something was hampering his efforts. Perhaps she'd figured out a way to escape the images he'd been channeling. In any event, his new friends would know what to do.

From out of the corner of his eye, he saw something stirring the debris that littered the far reaches of the room. The things that walk between had departed, leaving him to himself and his new companions. A nervous twitter escaped him. Oh, yes! They could really sneak up on you! Slithering through the glowing mists, they whispered and snuffled, flowing and flapping toward him. He'd had lots of practice with hallucinations, but this was different; these images didn't go away in the blink of an eye or a shake of the head. Oh, no! They stayed around to get to know you! Not that it bothered him; they were his friends, his new friends, and, anyhow, his life had been so empty until they'd appeared. Giggling in delight, he allowed their feelings to fill him once more, letting the miasma of their thoughts seep into the spaces of his naked self.

The exchange was brief and, as the beings left him, he felt reinvigorated. His friends would provide what was needed; they would show him the way.

A noise distracted him from his silent musing. Snapping his head around, he focused on the large, jagged hole that he'd torn in the side of the attic wall. There, a diminutive figure, swaddled in shadows, was dancing silhouetted in the outline of the rupture. The splintered, fractious maw of the portal outlined the desiccated, leathery shape with ominous clarity. It was his first 'born' child.

And he was juggling.

Zak laughed, latching on to the astounding scene with the keen observance of a captive audience. His son was scampering and dancing about, juggling three whirling, white spheres. Leaning forward, he peered through the hazy darkness of the room, beginning to laugh harder as he caught onto the significance of the jugglery. The beautiful, white whirling balls were skulls. Very small skulls, to be sure, but skulls nonetheless. Delightful!

He knew what it meant. It meant 'two, by one, means three.'

Pulling the dirty black robes tighter about his lithe frame, he leaned forward and then carefully placed the book in the center of the diagram. Getting to his feet, he climbed through the hole and crossed the shadowy attic heading for the stairs. He knew he had better hurry; he didn't want to miss all the fun! Chortling to himself, he hurried down the hall, his hideous son scampering along beside him.

Day Three
Friday, April 29th, 1988
-6-

Mark Cook burrowed his hands deeper into the pockets of his denim jacket as he stared at the dilapidated old house. It was much bigger than he'd expected, the flaking, gray walls clawing their way up to the archaic, gabled roof in a grasping attempt to form an impressive, if not altogether sound-looking abode. He felt the light touch of goose bumps drawing across his skin as he stood scowling at the sinister spires and turrets. There was something tugging at the back of his mind, an undefinable tingle of warning perhaps, but he sealed himself off from the nagging uneasiness. He would let nothing distract him from his chosen task. There was too much riding on this for him to fail.

Pulling out a joint, he leaned back against a gravestone. Then, after snagging a lighter from his back pocket, he sparked the doobie to life, still eyeballing the structure in mild trepidation. Inhaling deeply, he allowed a slow smile to creep across his rugged features as he passed the spliff off to Rob.

Rob Thorn took it with a practiced ease, the nimble fingers of his other hand brushing strands of curly, blond hair out of the way so he could take a drag without bursting into flames. He gestured with the burning end of the joint as he exhaled a huge cloud of fragrant smoke.

"Are you sure we should be doing this?" he asked, "I mean, this is breaking and entering, you know."

Mark snorted. "Two 'puss' demerits, Rob, 'ole buddy. We're going in, and none of your pathetic whining is going to change that."

"Hey, calm down, Mr. Macho. I'm just stating the obvious. Just like it's obvious that little wench is pullin' you around by the chain."

Mark allowed his brows to crumple inward, head tilting to one side as his eyes locked onto his friend with a sharp, predatory look. It had the desired effect; Rob took a step back, holding up his hands in mock surrender.

"Don't get me wrong," he clarified, darting another glance at the graveyard dwelling, "I want to go in as much as you do. Hell, it'll be loads of fun." Handing the joint back he concluded, "That's if we don't get arrested. . ."

"Look, you weenie," Mark sneered, "you know how I feel about Kelly. She wants this set up, and I'm gonna get it done. The cops don't patrol around here no more and this place is totally abandoned. Let's just get on with it and. . ." Pausing, he took a copious hit, his voice finally squeaking out around the huge lungful of smoke, "have a few laughs."

Grinning, he passed the joint back, studying Rob's face. He knew his friend wouldn't wuss out on him. Rob was the kind of guy who always did what he felt like, no matter what the consequences. But now, after his last few run-ins with the law, he was trying to practice more self-control. Sticking the joint in his mouth, Rob dusted off the front of his black leather jacket and then grabbed the backpack resting by his leg.

"Well, come on then—I didn't skip school this morning to hang out with the dead. Let's find a way inside and set up Kelly's little party so we can get the hell outta here."

Mark laughed, slapping his companion on the back.

"Let's rock and roll then! Once we get inside and set up all this stuff, Kelly will be all mine. . ."

Rob snorted. "You think she's gonna let you get anywhere just for this? Ha! Better guys than you have tried. She just wants you to make a fool of yourself so she can lead you on some more."

"You don't know shit!" Mark snarled back, rounding on his friend. "She's been looking at me different these past few days. You just wait and see."

"Yeah, but does she give good head, is what I want to know. . ."

"Shut your filthy mouth!" Mark cried, eyes going a little wild. "A girl like Kelly don't do things like that. She's sweet and sophisticated. Don't even say shit like that about her!"

They came around the side of the building and Rob pulled up short.

"Did you hear that?" he whispered, his iron-hard fingers digging into Mark's shoulder.

"What?" Mark gasped, trying to look in all directions at once.

"Your pansy heart doing flip-flops, lover boy!"

Mark snatched the joint away from him. "Well, I may be a 'pansy lover boy', but I'm also the one with the weed, so you better cut out the bullshit if you want any more of this!"

They grinned at each other, then broke into delirious laughter, fragrant smoke swirling around their heads like a cloud of fluttering gray butterflies. Continuing onward, they soon came across a small door at the back of the house.

"This should lead to the basement," Rob said, setting his pack down and pulling out a crowbar.

"Yeah, but someone's already made us an easy entrance."

Bending down, Mark pulled at the bottom of the warped wooden door panel. It bent away from the siding, peeling back from the frame to expose a triangular gap wide enough to crawl through.

"Lem'me see the flashlight. . ."

Rob handed it to him and they eased through the hole on hands and knees, letting the flap slap closed behind them. It was darker inside than he'd expected. At seven o'clock in the morning some light should have been getting through, but the stairwell they found themselves in was as black as the shores of midnight. The flashlight didn't shed much light in the encroaching gloom, but they were just able to make out their surroundings.

The walls were covered with brown and green lichens and the old wooden stairs appeared cracked and wormy from many years of disuse. As they started downward, the dank air clung to them, bringing the sharp, unpleasant odor of decay. It was not a very welcoming place. In fact, Mark thought, it's downright creepy.

Reaching the bottom of the steps, he shined the pitiful light around. They were in a large, rectangular chamber with a high ceiling made up of old, prehistoric-looking timbers. From where they were standing, they could see it was filled with rotted boxes and ancient, shroud-covered furniture. Mark winced at the harsh sound of Rob's sudden laughter.

"Looks like they didn't get rid of it all at the 'yard sale'."

"Yeah," Mark breathed, trying not to taste the fetid air, "this place is nasty."

"Hey, what's that?"

Shining the flashlight upward, he scanned the ceiling arches, viewing what appeared to be long, voluminous sheets of silk.

"Holy shit," Rob whispered. "Look at the size of those cobwebs!"

"Yeah, I see 'em. . . "

Mark reached around behind himself to pull a baseball cap from his back pocket. Shoveling a hand though his thick, black hair, he scrunched it down onto his head.

"That's better; I don't want to get any of that crap in my hair. Let's get going. I want to get this over with so I can visit Kelly during lunch. Won't she be surprised when we tell her that everything's ready for her little shin-dig?"

"Yeah, and won't they all be surprised when they discover our own little additions?"

Dissolving into laughter, their peals of mirth echoed throughout the darkness. What they'd planned for the girls would be a great deal more exciting than just some run-of-the-mill scavenger hunt; it would be a monument to thrill seekers everywhere. Removing their packs, they started working their way toward the opposite end of the house, passing the roach back and forth and joking around as they did so. It was sure to be one hell of a weekend indeed.

***

They were about halfway done setting things up when they stumbled upon the rat, but it didn't really look like any rat they'd ever heard of. Its body was mostly hairless and also quite malformed.

"Whew! What an ugly bugger!" Rob breathed, pushing a discarded beer bottle over for a size comparison. "Look how huge it is! It looks like a goddamn beaver."

"Yeah, and take a gander at those teeth! I wonder if this is some kind of new species? Maybe it only lives near graveyards."

"Come off it, Mark. There hasn't been a fresh corpse around here in ages; what would it eat? It's probably some kind of muskrat or something."

"Well, whatever it is, it didn't die happy—check out its stomach!"

Rob leaned down, playing a splash of light over the rodent's midsection. "Wow! That looks like a friggin knife wound. I wonder who would be crazy enough to go around cutting up something this freaky-looking? I know that I wouldn't want to find one of these critters alive; I mean, just look at those teeth!"

Mark studied the creature a moment more, silently agreeing with his friend—it would definitely be a very bad idea to tangle with something like this were it alive and kicking. An icy chill ran through him.

"Maybe we ought to go tell Kelly about this," he said slowly. "I don't think she'd have much of a good time if there are any more of these things around." Not to mention, he thought, whatever had done it in.

"Come on, lover boy," Rob quipped, "remember Kelly? Those smooth, soft legs, that slender, silken neck, those firm, ripe—"

Mark took a playful swipe at his friend. "Watch it, buddy! You're talking about the girl of my dreams there!"

Laughing, Rob danced back out of the way. "Whoa, I'm like, really scared. 'Please, mister big, bad, barroom brawler, don't hurt me or nothin' like that'."

Mark chuckled at his friend's bad impersonation of Jerry Lewis. He was such a clown, but he was right; this thing probably crawled in here to die. The stomach gash could have been made by anything, and as for the chew marks, maybe a cat or something. Anyway, disappointing Kelly was not on his list of things to do today. Pushing the feelings of unease to the back of his mind once more, he cleared his throat.

"Yeah, well, let's just leave it here. They gotta come this way to get to the rest of the house, and it'll scare the shit out of them. Let's get going on the rest of the stuff, though; I want to finish with the upstairs and get back before lunch."

"You mean, 'get back to my darling, Kelly,' don't you?"

"You're asking for it, Rob—just keep it up. . . "

"Oh, you're so tough! When I grow up, I want to be just like you!"

Trading insults back and forth, they worked their way

around to another staircase, this one leading upward. The basement was now completely rigged, and the scavenger hunt items all placed as ordered. Their own embellishments guaranteed that there would be plenty of girlish screaming during the upcoming weekend, and, taking a last look around, they started up the stairs toward the hallways above.

It was as they reached the second landing that they heard it. It was a soft, scrabbling sort of noise, accompanied by a slithery hissing sound. Within moments, they found themselves surrounded by a glowing mist that sprang up out of nowhere. It curled around them, roiling, clinging, and brushing across them like an unwelcome lover. They cried out, bumping into one another in an effort to flee, but there were things in the mist, strange, coiling, half-formed shapes, that prevented their escape. As they were swallowed up by the haze, they heard a repellent voice barking out harsh commands in an unfamiliar tongue.

From deep within the dwelling, their screams rose to such a fevered pitch, that, had there been anyone around to hear it, it would have been the cause for deepest concern. But the graveyard remained deserted. A chilling wind blew among the stones, lifting leaves and debris with its gentle touch and scattering them in small whorls about the long unattended grounds. The screams slowly faded with the sighing of the breeze and, once again, the house fell silent.

-7-

Williams hadn't slept very well and he doubted that he ever would again. He'd broken his own personal code of ethics by lying to the LePrades. How could he live with himself now knowing that he'd only prolonged the problem instead of correcting it? Then again, how could he correct it? He simply could not see himself involved in something so horrifying and dangerous. After all, what could a small town psychologist do to help them out of their dilemma? There was nothing, nothing that he could do. . .

There had to be something.

Sighing, he leaned back in his chair. He'd gotten to the office early after being unable to find sleep at his small, suburban home. He was jumping at shadows and thought that getting a head start on the morning might help to calm his nerves. It hadn't. His mind kept going over what had happened in his office the previous day. Shaking his head to clear it, he glanced down at his hands. The right one was fiddling with a pen, the left, now bandaged and still throbbing, was cradling a lumpy object. Setting the pen down, he gazed at the remains of his watch. She had melted it down to slag. Or, 'it' had. And whatever that thing was, it had made him a believer. Now, for the first time in his life, he actually believed in the supernatural. He was still in shock because of it.

Putting the remains of the watch away in a drawer, he turned and tapped the intercom button.

"Oh! Good morning!" came Terry's familiar voice, "I didn't know you were in so early."

"Yes. Well, I couldn't sleep. Will you please reschedule all my appointments for today? Also, bring me a cup of coffee, black. A large cup."

"But you don't drink coffee!"

"I do now. Just get it for me, okay? Please?"

"Sure thing, Doc. Coming right up."

The intercom clicked off. Leaning back again in his chair, he smoothed his rumpled tie and tried, without much success, to think of a solution. After a few minutes, Terry came in. She was beautiful, as always. This morning she was wearing a soft, brown shirt and a pair of black slacks. Her long, silken hair was pulled back into a loose braid, and her black boots made small scuffing sounds as she crossed the hardwood floor. Her face wore a look of deepening concern as she placed the coffee in front of him.

"Is there anything wrong?" she ventured.

"No. . . Yes! I don't know. . . " he faltered. "I. . . I just don't know anymore."

Terry gazed at him a moment, taking in his disheveled condition as he grimaced around a large gulp of coffee. "You don't look so good, Doc. You want to talk about it?"

"I can't; it's about a patient. Confidentiality and all that."

Sitting down, she quirked a smile at him. "Well, you do realize that whatever you say to me won't leave this office? Ever since I started working here, you've treated me more like a colleague than a receptionist. In fact, you've been almost like family, and, although you may not realize it, I consider you one of my closest friends. No, no, wait. . . let me finish!" With a wave of her hand, she cut off his half-formed demurral. "You work very hard at what you do, and you're damned good at it. I've really learned a lot from watching you handle your patients and it's made me decide that it's what I want to do when I graduate. Help people, I mean.

"Now, I can tell there's something bothering you, something disturbing enough to make you cancel all your appointments and start drinking a beverage you completely despise. Why don't you get it off your chest? It will make you feel better. And, if it helps, you can think of yourself as my first real patient. What do you say?"

He gazed into her deep brown eyes and found nothing but compassion there. He'd already broken his own code of ethics; what was one more infraction? Besides, this thing was eating him up inside. He had to get it out in the open so he could meet it head-on and resolve it. It was the only way.

If she'd only believe him.

Slowly, and with many false starts, he told her about the horrifying events of the previous day. All the terror of what he'd witnessed, all the monstrous implications, all the deception he'd propagated—he told her everything, everything and more. He began to tell her what he thought of himself for deceiving his patients this way, but Terry interrupted.

"There was nothing else you could have done. Prescribing sleeping pills, in any event, was probably a stroke of genius. It will buy us some time to work out what we're going to do."

Startled into near speechlessness, he managed to sputter, "What we're going to do?"

"Certainly," she said, leaning forward. "You're going to need help in finding out the best way to diffuse this situation. You forget, I've taken a couple classes in parapsychology, and while I know this should all be sounding crazy to me, I totally believe you. Trust me—I've studied a lot stranger cases than this. But we're going to need to do some heavy research to find out what we're up against. You know we have to do this;

if not for the girl, then for your own peace of mind. Once we put this thing to rest, I think you'll feel a lot better. Now come on, let's get your coat and head downtown. We've got a lot of work to do."

"Where are we going?" he managed, still stunned by her ready acceptance and sincere offer of help.

"This town, you might not realize, has a dark history. I'm sure you've heard the rumors, haven't you?"

He shook his head.

"Well," Terry continued, listing them off on her fingers, "there have been disappearances, unsolved murders, unexplained events; the list just goes on and on. You'd be surprised. Also, there's all those old stories about that graveyard over on Mercury Street. Maybe we can find out if there's been any other occurrences like this in the past. Now come on; we've got to get to the library and try and dig up some more info. It could take us a whole day just to check the backdated news files."

Suddenly at a loss for words, he allowed himself to be pushed along as she hurried him into his overcoat and then out the door. They reached the parking lot and she hesitated.

"Do you want me to drive?" she asked.

He peered at her small VW Rabbit. It was hot pink and had fuzzy dice hanging from the rear view mirror.

Clearing his throat, he led her toward his shiny, black Buick Century. "No, that's okay; I'll drive. You know, you really don't have to do this. It's not your problem, and it could get pretty dangerous. Maybe you should just stay out of it."

"No way, buddy. This is my first chance to crack open a real occult case. Plus there are lives at stake here! Besides, it became my problem the moment you told me about it. We've got to stick together on this; there's strength in numbers."

Williams opened the passenger door for her and then moved around to the driver's side. He was worried for her safety, but, at the same time, relieved to have her support. He had to admit that he was also quite flattered. It was a boost to his self confidence that he was sorely in need of.

As they drove through town, he reflected on what Terry had said about the strange goings on she'd heard of. This old town didn't seem like the kind of location that could harbor any hidden secrets. It was just a tiny little place on the border of California and Arizona, hardly even a pimple on the face of America. The people were friendly enough, for the most part, and he certainly didn't have any knowledge of these supposed mysterious occurrences. Still, he trusted her —needed to trust her—and she'd never given him any reason not to.

Sighing, he continued to drive toward the south side where the Pritchford Library was located, noticing the everyday bustle of the small community. People were walking along the sidewalks, ordinary people, moving with a purpose in their daily lives. This was a town of simple, hardworking folk, not some place out of a Steven King novel. Glancing at Terry, he had to wonder. Even though he'd witnessed the reality of the LePrade girl's. . . 'possession' he guessed he should call it. . . he still had trouble assimilating his new found beliefs. They were not something he'd thought he'd ever have to deal with. For God's sake, he was a psychologist, not a witch doctor! But Terry had accepted his version of the events without even blinking an eye. He supposed that he would just have to get used to it.

They pulled up to the library. It was a large, red brick structure that resembled a fallout shelter more than an institute of learning. The construction aside, it was very functional and held thousands of books. He'd visited there many times, although not to investigate anything of this magnitude. For all he knew, this evil he'd stumbled upon could involve more than just the LePrades; it could very well affect the whole town. It was an earth-shattering realization that was only now beginning to sink in. Taking a deep breath, he firmed his resolve, then stepped from the car.

The day was mild but growing increasingly warmer. That was the way of things this close to the desert: freezing cold at night, and hotter than hell during the day. Thinking back, however, he was surprised to realize that the weather had been unusually chilly for this time of year. Normally, it got up into the nineties on the average. This season, it was still a brisk sixty-nine degrees, the wind seeming to hang on and regroup as it forced its way through the streets, sometimes howling well into the night like a beast of prey stalking out new territory. It was a very disturbing thought that added to his growing sense of unease. There was something strange going on in Plentsville, and he was right in the middle of it. It gave him an almost uncontrollable urge to cut out of there, just drive away and never look back.

"Okay, Doc, once we get inside, we'll research the news archives, then try to access the town records. It could be tricky if they're sticklers for protocol, but it should at least give us plenty of room for speculation. At least it'll be a start."

Gazing at Terry, he knew he couldn't run from this; she was counting on him. Also, there was Robin to consider, and perhaps the safety of the entire town. Like it or not, he was going to have to play the hero for a while.

He found that he did not like it at all.

-8-

The interior of the library was as spacious as the exterior suggested. Rows upon rows of bookshelves stood at rigid attention, the soldiers of knowledge waiting to serve in mankind's never-ending battle to learn. Moving through the heavy silence of the lobby, they approached the desk where Mrs. Howards was on duty, her graying hair pulled back into a severe bun. She peered at them over her horn-rimmed glasses with a face as sour as day-old lemons. It would seem that she didn't approve. Then again, she hadn't approved of much of anything for as long as Williams could remember. He tried to keep his temper in check; it wouldn't do any good to antagonize the old busybody. Flashing a smile that did not quite reach his eyes, he greeted her with a strained civility.

"Ah, hello, Mrs. Howards. We'd very much like to see the newspaper archives, please."

"Won't do you any good," she replied tartly.

Wincing, he tried again. "But surely it's okay for my associate and I to look over the back-dated news files? We won't be needing to—"

"I said it won't do you any good," she cut in. "Mr. Volendorf, the archivist, is out of town. He has the only other key."

"The only other key?" he prompted.

"Well, of course, being the head librarian, I retain

53

copies of all the keys to the premises, from the town records on down to the storage lockers. But Mr. Volendorf is in charge of that department, and he won't be back until Monday. I'm terribly sorry, but you'll just have to wait until he returns."

"But surely you can—"

"Certainly not! Dr. Williams, you don't think I would break library policy just so you and your. . . assistant. . . can search through some old newspaper files, do you?"

"Mrs. Howards," he began again, starting to lose his patience.

"Let me handle this," Terry whispered, easing past him.

Facing the desk, she stared the older woman straight in the eyes. "Mrs. Howards, you are the head librarian, correct?"

"Yes, but—"

"And part of your duties as the librarian is to facilitate the access of resource material to people like us with a legitimate reason to be here?"

"Well, of course, but—"

Softening her voice, she reached across and took one of the old woman's hands. "Then please allow us to go through the news archives, just this once. I assure you the information we seek is vital and it's imperative that we get to it today."

"Well," the old woman sniffed, glancing down at the hands now encircling her own. "Since you put it that way, maybe I can bend the rules a little just this one time. Come with me, and I'll show you where the microfiche room is located."

Following her through the maze of towering bookshelves, they reached the back of the library and descended a carpeted stairwell. The lighting was irregular and dim in the musty corridors of the lower levels, and Williams stifled a sneeze as he followed after the two women. It wasn't long before they came to a door labeled 'Archives'.

Using the master key, she unlocked it, then turned to them. "Now, you best be about your business and leave quietly afterwards. I'll tolerate no shenanigans in my library!" With that, she gave them such a look of reproach that it made him feel like a child caught with a hand in the cookie jar.

"Wait," Terry said as she turned to go. "What about the town records; we'll need the keys for those as well. . ."

"Don't push your luck, little missy!" came the vehement response. "Those require the proper forms and the proper clearance, of which you have neither."

Terry gave a low growl of frustration as the librarian stalked away. With a small shrug and a roll of her eyes, she entered the room, moving her hand along the wall to click on the lights.

The hall of archives was immense. All along the back wall rested the microfiche storage indexes and, off to the left, stood locked cabinets containing the town records. In the center of the chamber were several large tables, two microfiche readers, and about a dozen or so chairs. To their right, up against the other wall, was a cluttered desk that probably belonged to the archivist.

Williams gave her a sardonic smile. "This may take a while. . ."

"Yup," she replied, grimacing as she glanced around. "This should just about eat up our entire afternoon."

"You know, you're pretty impressive. I can't believe you got that old hag to let us in here."

Terry flashed him a dazzling smile, running a smooth hand back across her thick, dark hair. "Well, when you've got it. . ." she drawled, arching an eyebrow.

He gaped at her and she burst out laughing.

"Come on, Doc! Didn't you see me slipping her the fifty?"

His blank stare turned to one of open disbelief. "You

bribed Mrs. Howards?"

"You bet I did, bud. When you've got to get somewhere fast, sometimes it pays to grease the wheels, know what I mean? Now, let's get started. You go through the newspaper files and try to find something we can use, and I'll go through the town records."

"But, we didn't get the keys," he protested.

Reaching into her bag, she pulled out a nail file. "I've got the keys right here," she stated, a dangerous twinkle in her eyes. "I grew up with four older brothers. You can learn a lot of useful stuff from being the youngest and watching all the troubles your siblings get into."

She threw him a challenging glance, as if to say 'you got a problem with that?' He didn't. Instead, he found himself grinning like a fool.

"You're absolutely amazing," he breathed.

"Is that your professional or personal opinion, Doctor?" she inquired playfully.

He felt his face grow flush. "A little of both, I guess. No offense?"

"None taken. You're pretty amazing yourself. Now, let's get moving; I don't want to spend any more time down here than we have to. There's no telling when that horrid old biddy will show back up, and I want to be long gone before that happens!"

He felt a little lightheaded at her compliment, but wasted no time in hunkering down to the job at hand. They searched through endless racks and cabinets of mostly useless information, and he was almost up to the current year in the news files when she suddenly flopped down across the table from him. Her normally sunny expression had faded and several strands of hair had come loose to hang about her face. With a barely suppressed yawn, he leaned his elbows on the table and peered across at her.

Easing back a little in her seat, she cracked her neck

and then stretched a bit. "Well," she said at last, "did you find anything?"

"A lot more than I expected, but not much of any use," he replied, gesturing down at the stacks of microfiche spread out before him. "There have been reports of missing persons and unsolved murders, but no mention of anything like what I've experienced. And none of this other stuff seems to be connected. Or at least not connected in any concrete way. . ."

Leaning toward him, she gave an impatient wave of her hand. "Anything could be important. Even the weakest link could be the start of a chain. Tell me what you've got, Doc."

"Well, there is this one thing. . ." He hesitated, not wanting to contemplate the significance of what he'd found, but realizing it could be their only lead. Clearing his throat, he plunged on. "I took down the locations of all the murders and unexplained events. It's most likely coincidental, but they all happened in the areas surrounding that graveyard. There were even a couple of letters to the editor complaining about all the strange goings-on up at that place. Unfortunately, it's all privately owned and the owners seem likely to remain anonymous."

Sniffing, she leaned back again, folding her arms across her chest. "You're right; that is pretty weak. That parcel of land has been around for so long that it probably marks the true center of town before the community expanded. This uptown portion was all built pretty recently." Sighing, she reached up to massage her forehead. "I came up empty too; there just isn't anything suspicious in the town records. Long story short, it's all pretty standard information for a town of this size. I did come across the name that's on the deed to that graveyard property; it was originally owned, and still is as far as I can tell, by the Jedidiah family. The land started out as a homestead and, after a time, became the town graveyard. The current owners aren't listed, of course, but one of the last ones is. His name was Ezekial P. Jedidiah."

Having grown more and more uneasy as she rattled on, his face suddenly went slack in dawning realization. Sweat beaded his forehead as he felt the room begin to spin out of focus.

"Hey, Doc! What's wrong? You've gone all pasty-faced on me. What the devil is the matter?"

Clearing his throat and trying to work some saliva back into his overly dry mouth, he choked out a reply. "Jedidiah. . . I. . . I know that name. . ."

She stared at him, concern coloring her features as she reached across to steady him.

"That name—it's the name of my patient's husband. The Jedidiah part, I mean. LePrade is a maiden name; it's the name that Carol went back to after the loss of her husband. Ms. LePrade was married to an Ezra Jedidiah."

It was Terry's turn to look shaken. "Oh my God," she whispered, "how did he die?"

"I don't really know; she's a fairly new patient and hasn't begun to comfortably open up to me as yet. But I bet we're going to find out before all this is over."

As the importance of the discovery sank in, his head was swimming with half-formed speculations. They now had a connection, however tenuous, but what did it all mean? Could the series of unexplained events have anything to do with his patients deceased husband? And, if so, how was Robin involved? Whatever the case may be, this did not bode well for their investigation. Well, they hadn't come this far expecting it to be easy; they'd come here searching for information that could point them in the right direction. It was the possible ramifications of this newfound knowledge that worried him. Now that they had a possible connection, what was their next move?

All at once a memory struggled up from the depths of his mind, something that had been subconsciously nagging at him all day.

"Nathrotep," he whispered.

"What?"

"Nathrotep. It's one of the words that Robin used when she was. . . possessed. She kept repeating it, chanting it. I don't know what it could mean."

"Nathrotep," Terry mused, scratching her chin as she gazed at the ceiling. "It could be some type of cult reference. Let's head over to the metaphysical shop across town and see if we can find out what it means. They have books over there that I seriously doubt we can find in this library. Come to think of it, now that we know the graveyard has a history, and that the LePrade's are somehow involved, maybe we should check out that abandoned house as well. . ."

Recoiling in surprise, he almost fell right off the chair. The last thing he wanted to do was go exploring up at that graveyard in the dark of night! She noticed his reaction and broke off what she was saying to give him a reassuring grin.

"Don't worry, Doc—we're not going near that place tonight. Let's just gather all the information we can find and then get some rest. Tomorrow, if we think we still need to, we'll go have a look then, okay? We might find something useful up there—you never know."

-9-

The store was a squat, rectangular building covered in peeling paint and moss covered shingles. It was an unusual location for a shop, being situated at the top of a hill on the far side of town, but it was far enough from the graveyard for Williams to relax a little. Pulling up to the curb, he turned off the engine, squinting up at the dilapidated structure.

"Well, it doesn't appear it's open," Terry said. "But let's go up and at least see what the sign says."

They climbed the rickety, wooden stairs leading to the battered front door. A hand-painted sign informed them that the place was called, 'The Source'. Raising an eyebrow at the colorful name, Williams tried the doorknob and found it unlocked. He opened it for Terry, then followed her into the shadowy interior.

Tall racks of books stood in the middle of a cramped room, while glass cases along the walls displayed all manner of occult paraphernalia. Letting his eyes adjust to the dim lighting, Williams moved toward the counter, trying not to breathe the cloying, incense-heavy air too deeply. Strange and somewhat bizarre items fought each other for shelf space, seeming to clamor for his attention as he moved between the rows.

He was studying a jar that contained what appeared to be a pickled cat, when the proprietor walked through an archway in the back. He was a swarthy man, balding and overweight, his remaining hair a tangle of greasy, black curls. The robe he wore made it seem like he'd been getting ready for bed.

"How you all doing this evening?" His voice rumbled with just a hint of a southern drawl. "The name's Jarrod. I was just about to close up fer the night, but is there something I can help you folks with?"

Eyes glistening in the flickering fluorescent lighting, he stepped up behind the counter, surveying them with unfeigned curiosity. As Terry moved forward, his gaze slid across her and he gave a low whistle of appreciation.

"Ma'am, you are the best-looking customer this ole shop has ever done seen. Begging your pardon, but I do mean that in the nicest possible way. . ."

His grin was bone white and large, crinkling up his face like a layered sponge cake. Williams stifled an angry retort; at least the man had good taste.

"Sorry to bother you so late," he began, "but we're in need of some information. We're hoping you can help us?"

"Shucks, son," came the jovial reply. "Go ahead and ask, and I'll give it a shot. I know quite a bit from running this here shop over the years, so you just tell me what you're looking fer, and I'll see if I can oblige you."

"Can you tell us the significance of the word, 'Nathrotep'?" Terry asked.

For a brief moment, Williams thought he saw a flicker of fear slide across the bulky man's features. Then, it was gone, replaced by a disarmingly toothy grin.

"Nathrotep, you say. Well, I ain't heard that one in years! Of course, it does have significance. The question is, do you really want to know? No, no. . . don't answer that; it ain't none of my business. I don't even want to know why you want to know."

Turning to the shelves behind him, he rummaged

around, and then took down a large book bound in crumbling leather. As he turned back, his eyes roved over them with intense scrutiny. Still, he didn't comment as he began flipping through the crinkled, yellow pages. Williams glanced at Terry to see if she was catching the proprietor's strange reaction to their request. She caught his eyes and gave an almost imperceptible nod of her head.

"Hmm, let's see here," the man said, scanning a page. "Yes, here it is—'Nyarlnathrotep'. Pretty nasty creature if ever I saw one. You all sure you want to hear this? Yes, yes of course; I can see that you do." He paused, taking a deep breath, then continued. "This here's a very dangerous entity. It's said he can manifest himself in over a thousand different ways—"

"But what exactly is he?" Terry broke in.

"What you all got yourself here is one major old world deity, folks. I don't know what you two is wrapped up in, but, iffen I was you, I'd run the other way. You don't want to be messing around with anything associated with this; it just ain't safe."

His piercing gaze made the hairs on the back of Williams' neck stand up. The man was trying to warn them off, that much was obvious, but what he was telling them sounded like complete nonsense. Only now, after what he'd witnessed with the LePrade girl, he was willing to consider any information, however outlandish, that might be of some use to their investigation.

"Please," Williams urged. "We need to know more about what we're mixed up in. I won't go into detail, but I will tell you this; we're in the middle of something that's beyond our understanding. Anything you can tell us will be a great deal of help."

Clearing his throat, the man turned the book over in his hands, giving their request a great deal of careful consideration. At last he let out an explosive breath, running a chubby hand over his balding pate. "Well, iffen you got to know, then you got to know. But don't say I didn't warn you." Glancing down, he reopened the tome and began to read silently, his lips moving as he took the information from the book and translated it into English. Williams didn't recognize the writing as he peered over the counter—it appeared to be gibberish. Obviously, it was not.

"Nyarlnathrotep, or 'Nathrotep', as you're calling him," he began, "well, what you got there is the heart and soul of the 'outer gods' in the pantheon of the Sumerian mythology —the Crawling Chaos, as he's sometimes called. Strange beings, these outer gods are; evil and demented through and through. It's said that their messenger is this here Nathrotep, and that he brings madness whenever he's invoked. He's also prophesied to be the harbinger of doom to the human race. The cults that worship him are a secretive bunch, but their power and influence is undeniable.

"It's a very dangerous type of business you're interested in, and not the kind of thing I'd 'spect two honest, bright, young people such as yourselves to go fooling around with. . ."

Williams had become more and more apprehensive as he'd listened to the shop owner's explanation. Just what in the hell had they gotten themselves into? Trying to process this newfound knowledge was only giving him more unanswered questions. Just what was this supernatural figure, and how did it fit into what was happening to Robin? This was not the type of thing that any sane person would choose to get more involved with. Still, there was no one else they could turn to. Perhaps they would also need to search that graveyard property after all, if only to discover more about how it was connected to his client. Anything that could lead them to discovering what had happened to his patient's daughter might be well worth the effort. But just thinking about it made him cringe inwardly. As if reading his thoughts, the proprietor suddenly broke the silence.

"You all are thinking about going up to that ole house, ain't you?"

Startled, Williams felt a sickening wave of fear surge within him. "How did you know that?" he blurted.

Jarrod seemed to pull into himself, standing taller and somehow managing to appear like an entirely different person. The lights continued to flicker above him as his face took on an air of grim severity. It was an eerie transformation and Williams couldn't help himself from taking a step back, Terry gripping his forearm in support.

"I know many things," he began, his voice hard edged and somehow colder than before. "If you're going on up there, then you should be warned. That house is an evil place. Lots of strange things happening around there. I suppose you all done heard about some of them things or you wouldn't be planning to do what you're thinking on doing now."

"We. . . we know there's been a lot of unusual events in that area," Terry offered. "We've read through some old news files at the library. . ."

"Then you should also know this: over the years I've come to discover there's a series of tunnels that run all beneath that place. Down in them tunnels you may find some things you don't want to see. Things that shouldn't be there— things that live down there in the darkness. When you were over at the library, did you notice anything funny about the dates?"

"Dates?" Williams asked faintly.

"Them disappearances and such. All them unexplained occurrences seem to happen at certain times of the year. Times when the planets align, times of the solstices, a lot of certain, significant times. Tomorrow night's the thirtieth of April; this be one of those times. It's a good night fer it, I suppose. A mystical night when the powers of Earth are strong and the stars have great influence."

Williams shuddered as he realized the man was right. Thinking back, he could remember many of the articles he'd read. A lot of the events had happened around the same times of year. Some of the worst ones had happened around April thirtieth. He hadn't realized the connection until now, and it chilled him to the bone. A slight dizziness overtook him and he grasped the edge of the counter to steady himself.

"These. . . things. The ones you mentioned," he ventured. "What are they? Could they be behind these strange goings-on, all the. . . unexplained events? Do these things. . . do they have the ability to possess someone's mind, to somehow control them?"

Jarrod hunched forward, his voice dropping to a near whisper. "The things that live beneath that site are abominations; who knows what all they can or can't do? I've been told that they tend to inhabit places such as this. Now, I ain't never seen one up close; just never had the gumption to go a lookin' fer 'em, you understand. But I know they're there. Creeping through them dank, old tunnels, living, breeding. . . and waiting. For what, I don't rightly know. But they're there alright. From what I've been able to find out, they don't stray much from that place. Something's holding them there, something dark and powerful. Just what it could be, I can't say fer sure. But I will tell you this: if you're going on up there, fer whatever the reason, I suggest you all get yourself some protection." His glittering eyes spoke volumes.

"We have to go. . . we've got to find—" Terry began.

He cut her off with a wave of one pudgy hand. "Now, I done told you, I don't want to know the details. Damn well said too much already. I've been around fer a long time, maybe seen some things I ain't ought to have seen, but I'm smart enough to know I wouldn't a lasted this long if I'd went poking my nose into what's going on up at that place. So consider this fair warning." He hesitated, his features twitching with suppressed emotion. Then, with an exhalation that blew out his cheeks, he added, "But there is something more that I can do fer you—there are a couple items that you might find useful. . ."

Rummaging around behind the counter, he came up with a long, black box and a velvety pouch. Blowing the dust off of the box, he flipped open the lid, and then took out a peculiar device. It was about a foot long and slender, its length wrapped round by moldering leather. At one end there was a small, claw-like foot ringed by dirty black feathers, and two brass bells dangled from either side. It appeared to be some kind of ghastly wand.

"This may help, or it may not—I don't know fer sure. Don't ask me what it is, just take it. Remember to keep it with you always. If it works, they might let you alone, in case you meet up with them. Now, chances are, you won't even see 'em; like I said, they're a secretive bunch. But, this close to the thirtieth. . . well, they do tend to get a mite bit restless. Now this, on the other hand. . ."

After passing the wand-like thing to Terry, he carefully upended the contents of the pouch into his right hand. It was a large, white stone, circular in shape, with strange hieroglyphics carved along the edges. Some kind of star-like symbol was engraved across its face.

Even from where they stood, Williams could feel it radiating power.

"This," Jarrod breathed, "is a talisman which is said to close the gates that can sometimes exist between our world and the places beyond; an 'Elder Sign', it's called. A very powerful item indeed. I've been told that placing this inside such a gateway will seal it, stopping them things, and others like them, from coming through into our world. Now, maybe it will and maybe it won't—shoot, maybe you won't even need it. But you take it just the same."

Placing it back in its pouch, he handed it over to

Williams. It was unusually heavy and he could feel it vibrating with self-contained energy. This was all moving too fast, things getting so terrifyingly complex. He was not ready for this, not ready at all. Still, it was too late for second thoughts; his mind was made up, even if it meant that he was only digging his own grave. Wincing at the unintended mental image, he glanced back up at proprietor once more.

"I've never been a believer in any of this stuff," he began. "But the things I've witnessed in the last two days have really opened my eyes. This whole mess has gotten me completely terrified, but we have to go through with it; we have no other choice." Without conscious thought, he had taken Terry's hand as he spoke, clutching it tightly. "We're very grateful for all you've done, but let me ask you this— why? I don't mean to sound unappreciative, but you don't even know us. These items you've given us, these ancient, powerful things. . . they must be worth a lot to you. Exactly why are you helping us?"

Jarrod leaned back, his features suffused with an anguish so palpable that he seemed to shrink down under the weight of it. His eyes grew shadowed and distant as he absently massaged his chest just above the heart, as if by applying gentle pressure he could wipe away an unrelenting pain.

"I used to live near there, you know." His voice, wistful and soft, dripped with barely contained sorrow. "Bout eleven years back it were. I was in the carpentry business then— never even heard of a 'juju fetish', much less anything about all this other stuff." He waved his hand in a loose circle, a gesture that seemed to encapsulate the entire store. "Had me a real fine woman back then. She was the prettiest damn thing you ever did see, with hair like sunshine and eyes as clear and blue as the sky." He stood silent a moment, collecting himself, then continued. "She was a few months pregnant when we met, having just moved here after getting out of a bad relationship, but that didn't make no nevermind in my eyes, or in my heart. She was everything to me. Then, I come home one day and she was dead. Found her tied to the bed, mutilated. Some kind of ritualistic thing the cops were guessing later. On top of all that, the child within her was gone—taken from her poor body and never recovered! The cops never did find out what'd happened to it. They never found a damn thing!"

The agony rising in his voice was so profound that Williams almost cried out in shared misery.

"I couldn't understand it. Why had this happened? Why? What kind of person would do such a thing? There was nothing I could do, no way that I could bring her nor the babe back. But I had to do something. So I began to study the occult, all branches of it, everything I could find. And I studied this here town as well. I done found out more than I ever could a dreamed about that damn graveyard and its black secrets.

"That's when I opened this here shop. It was a real good way to start gathering things that might come in handy. Now, I don't dabble much in the arts myself; I just wanted to understand them, learn to protect myself, maybe find a way to strike back one day. After awhile, all this forbidden knowledge that I'd collected sorta got to me, so I sold my house, moved in over here, and I've kept a respectful distance from that graveyard ever since.

"Now, I ain't no coward, I just ain't never been strong enough, you understand. No use getting yourself killed fer nothing, if you know what I mean. Now, finally, after all these years, I've been of some use. Maybe not directly, but, by helping you people, you two strong, committed, young folks, I can at last feel that I've done something useful, something that can finally make a difference."

The man was fierce in his defiance, his heated eyes boiling with internal passion. Normally, Williams would have considered him a bit unbalanced, but things being as they were, he practically saluted him. Here was a man with a big heart and, no matter what he said, he was the brave one here; all those years of living in torment, watching, gathering information and items that he himself could never use—it was quite impressive.

"We'll try and put these to good use," Williams assured him, tucking the elder sign into his pocket. "Perhaps we'll be able to return them to you when we're through."

Seeming to come back to himself, the man gave a ghost of a smile. "I am sure you will, friend, sure that you will. Now go on—get on outta here. It's time that civilized folk like me should be in bed. Perhaps I'll see you when you get done doin' what you gotta do. . ."

With that vote of confidence, they turned and departed the shop, both feeling a little stunned by the sheer enormity of the task that lay before them. It was going to be a lot more difficult than they both had imagined to unravel the rest of this mystery. Neither of them spoke much as they drove back toward the center of town, each wrapped up in their own private thoughts.

-10-

Robin had been forced to stay home from school again, and she was mad enough to spit nails. It felt like she was grounded, especially since she'd also been forbidden to go to Kelly's slumber party. It just wasn't fair! They were just nightmares, weren't they? She had the pills and everything was fine, wasn't it? But, no, her mother had to keep her in and coddle her like a damn baby. She was so humiliated she couldn't even bring herself to speak with Kelly, and Kelly had called twice!

Flopping down on her bed, she threw the television remote against the wall. It shattered, the small pieces flying everywhere as she looked on in utter disgust. Great. That was just the icing on the cake of her day. Now she'd have to get up and work the damn thing manually if she wanted to watch her shows. Fuming, she snatched the bottle of pills off the nightstand and rolled them back and forth across her palm. Well, she thought, at least I'm not having those damn dreams anymore.

Sighing, she wondered how long she'd be taking the pills; there seemed to be an awful lot of them. Gazing down at the bottle in her hands, she decided she had nothing better to do. Popping the lid off, she fished out two of the small, pink and white capsules. After a moment's hesitation, she shook out a third. After all, she wasn't going anywhere

71

tomorrow, so why not sleep in? Maybe that would give her mom one more thing to bitch about. Her lips twitched into a sour smile at the thought.

Taking a sip of water, she swallowed the pills, grimacing a little as they went down. Then, turning off the lamp, she hunkered down beneath the covers.

After drifting on the edge of sleep for about fifteen minutes, she heard a light tapping at the window. For a brief moment, she thought she was dreaming, but then realized she was still partially awake. Rolling over, she peered at the moonlit casement to see what was making the noise.

Outside her window, outlined by the moon's pale glow, was a figure. As her eyes adjusted to the light, she realized who it was.

Mark Cook!

It couldn't be. Maybe the drugs were screwing with her mind. Struggling to sit up, she ran trembling fingers through her hair, shaking her head a little, then looked again. It was him! With some effort she got out of bed, smoothing out her nightshirt as she crossed the room. Steadying herself on the sill, she opened the window and leaned out.

"Mark!" she whisper-shouted. "What are you doing here? My mom will kill me if she sees you!"

Mumbling something incomprehensible, he shifted from foot to foot as he stared up at her. There was something different about him, something strange, but he looked so good standing there in the moonlight. She caught herself gawking and hoped that he wouldn't notice her open appraisal. But he just stood there, his eyes, like deep pools of night, boring into her as he stretched out a tentative hand.

"I need. . . need to talk to you. . ." he murmured.

Glancing around, she decided not to waste this opportunity; he obviously had something on his mind and she was more than willing to lend him an ear. Maybe he and Kelly hadn't hit it off as well as she'd previously thought and he was here to drag information out of her—she was the 'best friend', after all. As far as she was concerned, he could speak with her all night! Grasping the proffered hand, she gave him a boost up.

As he clambered through the window, she saw that his pants were ingrained with dirt and his jacket was torn.

"What happened to you?" she exclaimed.

"Fell. . . I fell. . ." he rasped, his voice low and husky in the silence of the small room.

"Well, what did you want to talk about?"

She could feel the heat radiating off his body and, in the moonlight, his face seemed chiseled from pale stone like an old, Greek statue. Her heart skipped a beat as he returned her frank stare, but still he said nothing, just stood there gazing at her with an inquisitiveness that was somewhat unnerving. After what seemed like an eternity, he reached out, his hand hesitant and unsteady.

"Robin. . . " he managed, his fingers trailing across her cheek.

His touch was like molten fire and goosebumps erupted all across her quivering body. It was becoming difficult to breath. What was he doing? It was almost as if he were seeing her for the very first time, his eyes were so searching, so. . . flattering.

With languid ease, his hand glided to the curve of her neck. Still, she couldn't take her eyes away from his face; every exquisite detail was outlined in unnatural clarity. She was captivated.

Tracing two fingers down the length of her collar bone, he let his hand slip to her shoulder. It sent shivery impulses coursing through her. With a glacial slowness, the fingers slid around, easing themselves down the smooth contours of her back. Light as a feather, they crept across the soft material of her nightshirt until they reached the gentle curve of her hip. Still gazing deeply into her eyes, he leaned forward, his free hand encircling her waist. Filled with soaring emotions, she melted willingly into his embrace. Here was what she had always longed for, and, as his lips brushed against her own, she was swept away, riding on waves of giddy delight.

Then, the pills overcame her, and she swooned.

Lifting her in his arms, Mark stepped to the window and jumped out. Landing with a bit of a stumble, he righted himself, then strode off toward the darkness of the graveyard beyond.

***

Zak stood in the center of the diagram, the wraith-like creatures swirling around him as he chanted. Rotating about his filthy body, never more than half there, his friends slithered and hissed as he worked the dark, pulsating incantation from the book of the dead. It was a lot harder than the previous spells he'd uttered, but the diagram was much bigger now, much stronger, and it was working; the words were having their desired effect.

He could feel the entranced thoughts of the boy as he moved closer, coming across the shadowy graveyard after completing his task. As he finished the last sentence of the malignant, power-infected chant, Zak began to laugh. Softly at first, as he watched the agitated writhings of the mystical, snake-like beings, then with more and more gusto, until he was gibbering and bellowing out in hideous joy. Now his friends would begin to show him new things, more powerful things, and he would be taught the secrets of the tunnels below. He longed for the chance to test his new-found strength and to call to the minions that slunk and hid beneath the graves. They seethed in the darkness, masses of them, awaiting his summons, and he knew that he'd be torn to pieces if he wasn't ready.

But, he thought with savage intensity, still screaming

out his mirth, I am ready. Oh, yes! The power was his and he would soon begin to use it in earnest.

Laughing with a humor far beyond sanity, he spread his arms wide and then whirled around and around the chamber. As he twirled, his cadaverous son scuttled forth from the shadows to chortle and caper about his thin ankles, the mists parting and reforming around them with every passage. His sinuous friends danced with him, their insubstantial bodies swirling through and around him. Soon, they knew, he would set them free.

He would set them all free. . .

Day Four
Saturday, April 30th, 1988
-11-

For the sake of convenience as well as personal safety, Terry had stayed with Williams at his small, ranch-style home. After discussing their plans, each had attempted to rest while the other kept watch, but the enormity of the task before them made it difficult. It was their similar yet individual thoughts that plagued them, punctuated by the heaviness of much somber reflection.

As daylight began to stream through the living room windows, Williams sighed. He was sitting in an armchair watching Terry as she slumbered on the low, beige-colored couch. She was lovely, even more so as the thin sunlight played across her upturned face. As if somehow sensing his wistful admiration, she opened her eyes to regard him.

"What time is it?" she mumbled.

"About eleven."

"Whew!" she exhaled, climbing into a sitting position and running her hands through her hair. "Why'd you let me sleep so long? I thought we were going to get an early start this morning?"

"You looked like you could use the extra rest," he lied, hoping she wouldn't suspect that he'd been staring at her. "It's

77

going to be a long day, and we'll need all our strength to see this thing through."

Stretching with a huge yawn, she glanced around his sparsely decorated living room, then focused on his haggard appearance.

"You look like you could use some extra shut-eye yourself," she said. "Would you like to sleep a little more before we head out? I could make us something to eat and wake you when it's ready?"

Shaking his head, he shuddered as dream images flooded back into his thoughts. Resting had been almost impossible for him; demons and graveyards kept dancing through his mind every time he closed his eyes.

"No, that's okay," he said, shrugging off the disturbing visions. "Let's just get going; we can grab something on the way to the store."

They'd already planned out their approach; after getting some supplies they'd explore the abandoned house from top to bottom. Robin had mentioned that she'd seen someone in one of the upstairs windows, so that seemed the logical place to start. If they were lucky, they wouldn't even need to go near those damn tunnels. Just thinking about it made him decide something he'd been on the fence about all night.

With a nervous determination, he got up from the chair and walked to the closet at the end of the hall. As he rummaged around on the top shelf, he was acutely aware of Terry watching him from where she sat. Finding what he was searching for, he went back to the living room. With a feigned nonchalance that belied his mounting anxiety, he set the boxes down on the table. Blowing the dust off of the smaller package, he opened it and lifted out a handgun.

"My God!" Terry gasped and asked, "Where did that come from? I was thinking we'd need to purchase something for protection, but I didn't expect you to have a gun here at your house."

"Well," he hedged, setting the .44 auto mag down and beginning to load one of the clips, "I didn't want to mess with the hassles of buying weapons when I knew we already had some. Besides, we probably shouldn't do anything to alert the police, like trying to get guns quickly without going through proper channels. If we got caught, they'd never believe any of this stuff—they'd probably just try and lock us up."

Seeing the guarded look on his face, Terry placed her hand on top of his, stopping the methodical loading.

"Barnaby? What is it?" she asked, using his first name for the first time. "Something's troubling you, I can tell; something besides the obvious, I mean. Where did you get these?" She gestured to the long, unopened box as well as the handgun.

He glanced away in shame as all the monstrous self-doubts of his past surged to the forefront of his mind. He didn't want to tell her, didn't want her to know about his painful insecurities. Looking back, though, he saw only compassion in the softness of her deep brown eyes. With some reluctance, he decided that she had a right to know.

"My father gave them to me," he managed, gazing at the shiny metal of the gun's barrel as he traced a finger down its length. Clearing his throat, he tried again. "My father was in the army, from as far back as I can remember. He was a hard man, very disciplined. I hated him for it; he treated me like a solider instead of a son, always making me do things the military way. My childhood was filled with endless drills, hours at the shooting range, and countless surprise inspections. He was molding me for the army, you understand. He wanted me to follow in his footsteps some day."

She could see the deep sadness in his eyes, sense the pain in his every movement as he struggled with the memories. Not taking her hand from his, she nodded for him continue.

"When I was seventeen, I told him that I wasn't joining the army. I told him that I wanted to help people, not kill them. That didn't go over too well. He ridiculed me for it— said I was a coward and a traitor. My plans for the medical profession were such a betrayal to him that he redoubled his efforts to break me of the idea. He was. . . brutal. I finally had to run away. With the help of my grandfather, I was able to attend college. I threw myself into my studies, trying hard to overcome the feelings of uselessness that my father had knocked into me.

"Eventually, I succeeded and began to practice medicine part-time while still taking classes, always moving upward, always striving to show him that I wasn't a failure. But even after I started becoming successful, he still called me a coward. Said I wasn't good enough to be a 'real man'. These guns. . . they were a parting gift from him—his final attempt at setting me straight. Told me I ought to at least own a 'man's tools', even if I insisted on being a 'cowardly traitor'. I've never even fired them."

As he spoke, tears had sprung up in his eyes. Moving to sit on the arm of the chair, Terry put her arm around him.

"Well, you're not a coward in my opinion," she murmured. "It takes a greater man than most to stand up to a father figure like you did, and to hang on to your dreams without his support. He'd be proud if he could see you now; not many people would choose to do what we're about to do. Most people would have long since ran from it, fleeing the problem instead of doing something about it."

"That's just it!" he cried, gazing up at her. "I have to do this! Don't you see? If I give up now, I'll become the lowly coward he always saw in me—just another civilian traitor without a spine. I have to finish this, have to prove to myself that I'm more than that. We may be Robin's only hope of survival and, whatever it takes, even though I'm so scared I can hardly think straight, I have to help her. I've just got to!"

Terry pulled him into a half-embrace, resting her chin on the top of his head as she comforted him. After a few moments, she gently disengaged herself to once more perch on the edge of the sofa. Pointing to the longer box, she asked with a hint of her old playfulness, "What's in the big one, Doc?"

Regaining his composure with visible effort, he opened it.

"This is a 12 gauge combat shotgun," he replied with a watery grin as he lifted it from the box. "It holds ten rounds and it packs a punch. Or, so I've been told."

Smiling in return, she picked up the 44. "I think I'll take this one, if you don't mind; it looks like it might fit much better in my purse."

With a shared mutter of dark laughter, they continued loading the weapons, checking to make sure that each gun was in good working condition. They took their time at this, Williams going over the finer points of gun safety, neither of them in a hurry to head toward their fated destination.

-12-

"You had Mark do what?"

Kelly was thrilled by the incredulity on Marilyn's face. She'd been waiting to tell her so she could savor the moment. It was too perfect! Sitting up straighter on her four-poster bed, she grinned at her friend.

"I asked him to set up a scavenger hunt for us at the house on Graveyard Hill!" she repeated. "Robin's been having all these weird dreams lately, and I thought it'd be fun to spend the afternoon in a creepy old house searching for stuff and spooking each other out. It'll be great; you'll see! In fact, that's why Rob and him skipped school yesterday. They're going to call us when everything's set to go."

"But, Kelly," Marilyn said, flashing her a sidelong glance. "They should have called by now, right? The day is half over already."

Glaring, Kelly stifled the urge to strangle her. Marilyn Benson stared right back with dark, innocent eyes, the expression on her olive-hued face one of doubt with just a hint of scorn. That's Marilyn for you, thought Kelly, always the skeptic. Well, soon enough Shana would show up with her boundless enthusiasm, and then Marilyn would have to fall in line. Of course, they'd be forced to put up with Shana's childish babbling all day, but it was a small price to pay for free transportation. Shana had the only car, and besides, she always went along with Kelly's plans no matter what the cost. It was really kind of pathetic, but she was ridiculously loyal that way.

As if summoned by thoughts alone, Shana Fletcher came bounding up the stairs. Dressed in her blue and gold cheerleader outfit, she sprang into the room, her tanned, well-toned legs flexing as she assumed an open, athletic stance. Her bleach-blond ponytail swayed a little as she tilted her head to the side, her chest threatening to burst through the material of her shirt. It was that push-up bra again. Everyone could always tell when she was wearing it; it was so obvious! But Kelly had never been able to find a diplomatic way to tell her friend how tacky it looked. And in any case there was no sense pissing her off—she actually felt kind of sorry for her.

"Hey, guys!" Shana gushed, "You've got to see this new routine I learned!"

Oh, no! Kelly groaned inwardly, she's going to make us watch another stupid cheer! It wasn't as if they didn't appreciate their friend's ability, it was just that her repetitiveness was so. . . annoying. Watching Shana work her way through the intricate moves and gyrations, Kelly tried not to appear too uninterested. Risking a glance at Marilyn, she could see by the helpless expression on her roundish features that she was feeling the same. Sighing, she turned back to watch Shana complete the cheer.

Finishing the stunt with a spirited shout, Shana slumped to the floor, folding her long legs up underneath her. "Well," she asked, somewhat out of breath, "what do you guys think?"

"That's great," Kelly said, trying hard to find enthusiasm.

"Yeah, real good, Shan." Marilyn added.

"Well, it's not as easy as it looks; it took me eight tries to get this first part right, and that ogre Jerry keeps dropping me during our big finale! He's just not very good at it. I wish they'd let us switch partners, then I could get someone like Phil or maybe Neal. They're both amazing and super hot—"

"Speaking of good-looking guys," Marilyn broke in, "guess what Kelly's got planned for us today?"

Kelly threw her friend a sour look; she'd been hoping to spring the news herself. Oh, well, at least the announcement stopped what would have soon become an all-too-familiar, one-sided conversation about the cheerleading squad. For that, at least, Kelly was eternally grateful.

"What's up, Kel?" Shana asked.

Relating the story once more, Kelly went into greater detail as she warmed to the topic. As she explained how Robin had given her the idea by pointing out a person that she imagined seeing in the window of the deserted house, Shana became as excited as she'd hoped, instantly cutting off any further naysaying from the pessimistic Marilyn.

After a few more minutes of animated discussion, their conversation returned to the subject of boys. Marilyn's current lover was in college, and he'd given her a golden locket with his picture inside. Shana was instantly jealous, even though she was practically dating the whole football team, and much of the talk between the two of them soon revolved around dating in general.

Turning back to Kelly, Marilyn eventually asked, "Why aren't you and Mark a thing yet? Everyone knows how he feels about you."

"I don't know," Kelly said, fidgeting, "I guess because he's a little too nice. I want someone who'll add a little spice to the relationship. Mark is way too predictable; flowers and walks in the park are fine for some girls, but I like a man who can surprise me."

Her forthright statement caused a sudden, heated debate about the virtues of men and what made them so appealing. At some point during the conversation, Shana thought to ask Kelly why Mark hadn't called them yet.

"I don't know," she confessed, twining her fingers together as she stared down at her hands. "He should have called last night. He and Rob probably got bombed out of their skulls while they were setting it all up—you know what potheads those two can be!"

A voice drifted up from the bottom of the stairwell shouting, "Phone!" Flashing her companions a triumphant smile, she got up to go answer the call. The talk continued while she was away: a dissertation on relationships in general that was so engrossing they both were startled when Kelly marched back in and slammed the door shut behind her.

"What's up, Kel?" Shana gasped, her eyes going wide.

"Yeah, who was on the phone?" Marilyn added.

"I'll tell you 'what's up'!" Kelly fumed, her anger barely contained as she paced back and forth. "That bonehead Mark ruined the surprise—he's already told Robin all about the scavenger hunt! In fact, that was her just now on the phone. She sounded kind of funny, you know, like she gets when she's already pissed off? She said she was going over there right away, and I bet she has some surprises of her own in mind. We'd better get over there right now or we could miss out on everything! When I see Mark, I'm gonna kill him! He was supposed to call me, not go and blab to her!"

They got their stuff together in a hurry and left, jumping into Shana's small MG and racing off toward the graveyard. Low black clouds scudded across the sky as they drove. True night was still hours away, but the darkness that crept along the streets, filling it with menacing shadows, seemed to flicker and expand with a life of its own. It leapt and raced after and around the speeding car as if it knew that twilight would soon claim them all, but the girls took no notice of it's ominous warning.

-13-

It was around six pm by the time Williams pulled up to the graveyard and the clouds had long since turned the sky an unpleasant grayish-black color, roiling and churning with the threat of imminent rain. And with the uneven grave markers lurking beyond the crumbling, vine-encrusted walls, the house itself had taken on an added air of foreboding, crouching in the semi-darkness like a predatory animal tensing for the kill. Scanning the unwelcoming landscape, Williams swore in a soft undertone, wishing they hadn't taken so long to get the supplies. With his resolve quaking, he glanced at Terry to see how she was holding up.

She turned and regarded him steadily, her lips set in a thin, determined line. Then, holding his eyes with her own, she lifted the .44 auto mag and clicked off the safety. There was no turning back now; they were going into that house and they weren't coming out again until they found some answers.

The wind howled and moaned around them as they got out of the car, tearing at them with elemental claws and chilling them with more than just a drop in temperature. Together, they fought their way to the trunk, popped it open, then they lifted out their packs. Terry paused long enough to dig out the large, tactical flashlight that they'd duct-taped onto Jarrod's moldering wand. She studied it with lips curled in involuntary disgust, then, glancing over, raised a questioning eyebrow. Shrugging with feigned indifference, he shouldered his pack, then grabbed the shotgun and pumped a cartridge into the chamber. Taking that as a sign of readiness, Terry flashed the light ahead of them and led the way through one of the gaps in the wall, moving into the outer rows of overgrown headstones.

Following after, Williams glanced up at the abandoned structure. He imagined he could see an aura about it, a nimbus that surrounded the ancient dwelling with an almost imperceptible air of menace. He winced as he stared at it. It was a veritable monolithic presence, jutting up from the ground with its archaic ramparts reaching to the sky in timeless ferocity. Clenching the shotgun tightly, he scanned the area as they moved across the field of ancient death. He could sense the presence of something watching them from the deep, enveloping shadows, something that seemed to surround them on all sides with a supernatural awareness. Swallowing hard, he drew courage from their strength of arms, their unwavering resolve, and the confidence that comes with a sureness of purpose.

Above them, the violence of the building storm writhed and, as if summoned by his fearful glance, lightning flashed lengthwise across the heavens, striking somewhere far off in the distance. As he counted under his breath, thunder snarled, causing Terry to peer back at him with a face gone ashen in the twilight. He could tell that she was catching the same vibrations of otherworldly influences that he was. The image of the house, briefly illuminated by the flash of lightning, superimposed itself on the surface of his retinas, and he couldn't shake the sinking feeling of dread as the first sporadic puckerings of rain struck his cheek like a jealous lover. Jamming the gun tightly into the crook of his arm, he moved forward, focusing on the job at hand. All too soon, the locked front door of the building confronted them from out of the shadows. Gritting his teeth, he pulled a crowbar from his pack.

The ancient lock snapped under his attentions and he was surprised to find himself grateful. It's not as if I'll feel any safer inside, he thought, pushing the doors open with a nerve-wrenching squeal. It was just that being out in the open made him feel strangely vulnerable. Once inside he hoped he'd be better able to control his emotions. Pulling out his own flashlight, he took a deep breath, then entered.

They found themselves in a long reception hall. The air was stagnant, ripe with the smells of moldering wood, ageless dust, and other fragrances as yet indefinable. They jumped as lightning flashed once more from behind them, outlining the darkened hall with split-second clarity. It did nothing to lighten the mood, however, as they made their cautious way toward the staircase located at the other end of the corridor. It was an unpleasant place, with peeling paint covering the walls and piles of trash littering the blackened, hardwood floor. Although a few paintings were still in evidence, they could see that all of the artwork depicted unnerving scenes and dismal-looking people. Darkness ruled this place; they could feel it clutching at them as they moved up the stairs, their feeble beams of light cutting a narrow path through the shadows.

Resisting the impulse to search the second or third floors, they didn't even pause at the landings. It was their intention to go straight to the top, starting with the attic and working their way down. Although the house was large, he figured that it shouldn't take more than a couple hours to search the entire thing. As they moved upward, gusts of chill, night air slipped through unseen cracks to howl down the deserted corridors, making an ominous counterpoint to the pattering rain and swelling thunder as they neared the top of the final staircase. It was there that they began to notice an unpleasant odor. Choking, Terry stumbled a little, almost knocking them both down.

"Good God!" She coughed, covering her mouth with a bandanna she'd yanked from her pocket. "What is that horrible smell?"

"I don't know," Williams replied, wrinkling his nose in disgust and then straightening his glasses. "Maybe some animal died up here. . ."

Pulling the neckline of his shirt up to cover the lower half of his face, he moved forward, leveling the shotgun with trembling hands.

The smell worsened as they approached the attic door. It was creaking back and forth, its hinges shrieking out a message of warning that chilled them further as they crept along the deserted hallway. Reaching the door, Williams pushed it open with the barrel of the gun, moving his foot to stop its angry protests.

In the uneven light they could make out a room some thirty feet across. The ceiling, slanting down from the peaked roof, gave the impression of shrinking dimensions and, as they eased along the left-hand wall, they could see that the chamber was littered with debris, but otherwise quite empty.

Then they saw the hole.

It was ripped into the wall directly opposite them, the ragged splinters of the gaping wound suggesting that violent tearing had recently taken place there. They edged forward, trying to get a better look at their discovery, and the smell intensified, forcing them to breathe only from their mouths to keep from retching. A void loomed beyond the hole; some kind of hidden place that had held its secrets for long ages. Now, looking at the wooden splinters littering the floorboards, they could tell that it had recently given up whatever vile, long dead knowledge it had protected for so many eons. Williams clutched the shotgun more firmly and noted that Terry had moved off to the side, covering him as the beam of her flashlight illuminated the irregular opening.

There was something in there, something. . . unclean. And even though he knew he must now cross that unwholesome threshold, he was quite certain that he did not want to see what lay beyond it.

***

Zak was ecstatic.

The Children of the Graves had reacted far better than expected to his powerful summons and had accepted his generous offerings with relish, meeping and yammering in delight as they pledged to him their service. His powers were tremendous now, almost beyond imagining. Soon, oh, yes, very soon indeed, would he complete his part of the ritual, and then release all of the carefully hoarded power back over to his new master. He hugged himself as he sat in the darkened chamber deep beneath the house, the chamber that the Children had guarded throughout eternity. Candles began to wink on as the master completed another part of the complex working and a muffled scream echoed up from the altar stone. It made Zak laugh, sending peals of mirth upward into the limitless spaces above.

"Zak," came the harsh, yet vibrant voice, silencing his maddened cackle. "Your duties are not yet finished. You have done well to serve me, and soon you shall receive your reward."

Groveling forward on hands and knees, Zak licked at the feet of the mighty one, clutching at one thin ankle with a trembling hand.

"But first," the voice grated, "there are further tasks I would have you attend to. . ."

"Anything, Master! Name it and it shall be done!"

Slowly, a small hand descended to cup his chin, lifting it up so that his eyes were captured by the master's cold, hard stare.

"There are others above and one of them has that which cannot be permitted to come here; a symbol of ancient power worn around his accursed neck. Liberate it from him and destroy it, and then you shall be free to enjoy all the things that have been promised to you. Behold!"

The shadows parted as some of the malformed, canid-like Children scuttled across the floor bearing an old, dirt encrusted casket. His friends, their snake-like forms writhing in expectation, fluttered in and around the partially rotted box as the lid was pried loose by the Children's scrabbling attentions. Zak was mesmerized. Inside of the upright coffin rested the putrefied body of a young woman. A low, throaty sound escaped from her mummified lips as her arms stretched forward.

"Zaaa. . . kkkk. . ."

Weeping and choking on ragged sobs, he staggered to his feet, shoving past one of the hissing Children with no regard for his own personal safety.

"My love!" he managed to gasp, sliding into her embrace as the cadaverous form of their son scuttled about them in glee. After giving her a long, sensuous kiss, he disengaged, turning once more to prostrate himself at the feet of his master. Taking the outstretched hand, he held it with great reverence, gazing into the master's smoldering eyes with a face slackened by worshipful devotion.

"I will do what you ask, oh Great One! I will destroy the talisman he carries, even if I have to rip his head from his shoulders to get it!"

Gesturing for the others to back away, the master placed a hand on Zak's brow, sending further instructions into his maddened thoughts. Then, Robin LePrade smiled, the thin light of the candles tracing the lines of her distorted face as she gazed out at the 'family' she had reunited at long last.

-14-

Williams could feel his heart pounding as they approached the hole in the attic wall. Struggling against his near rampant fear, he squinted through half-fogged glasses while trying to steady his shaking hands. It was not going to be easy entering into that unwelcoming void. The stench pouring out of it saturated the air, worming its way through the thick material of his shirt. Glancing at Terry, he could tell she was having similar problems, the bandanna she'd tied around her nose and mouth even less a deterrent to the clinging odor. Standing just behind him, the flashlight shook in her grasp as she tried to keep the .44 steady with her other hand. Swallowing the dry queasiness in his throat, he edged forward with the shotgun at the ready, shining his own light into the rupture.

As he stepped over the jagged threshold, he took in the unusual dimensions of the room beyond. It appeared to be formed from the adjoining eves of the attic, creating a somewhat triangular shape, with the two sloping sides meeting in the far corner. Driven by some unknown compulsion, he crouched down to study the floor, and felt a tingling sensation erupt near his throat. The flashlight dropped from nerveless fingers as his hand flew up to clasp the pouch that hung there. It was warm and vibrant to the touch, as if tremendous amounts of energy had suddenly sprang to life within it. Leaning back, he scanned the area, eyes now widened in growing panic.

"What is it, Doc?" Terry's asked. "What did you find?"

Risking a glance back, he could see her dim outline just beyond the flashlight's beam. She was peering into the room, the gun held ready as she tried to see what was going on.

"It's. . ." he began, but the rest of the words died on his tongue. The tingling was growing stronger, pulling at his neck, trembling at an almost subsonic frequency. Retrieving the flashlight, he played the beam along the floorboards, illuminating what was drawn there. An acrid taste flooded his mouth as he rocked back on his heels, trying, without much success, to keep from gagging.

As Terry's light joined his own, her reaction coming as a frightened gasp, they were able to trace out the extent of the vile markings. The floor was covered in archaic diagrams, diabolical pictographs, and other obscene imagery. Overshadowing it all was a large pentagram. It covered the entire space, encompassing the lesser drawings with an air of perverse authority, running over, around, and through them, joining them as one. Williams caught his breath as the vibrations from the Elder Sign grew more powerful, pulsing at his neck like a living, breathing thing. All of the carefully orchestrated pattern was drawn in blood.

"My God!" Terry said. "Most of these symbols represent forms of the darkest arts. As for the rest, I just can't say; I don't know enough about the workings behind such things to be able to decipher them. If I wasn't so damn scared, I'd be excited about this discovery, but, things being as they are, I say we just get the hell away from here. This place is beyond evil."

Climbing to his feet, Williams turned to agree with her, but stopped as a sudden cascade of sound erupted around them.

It was a high-pitched, animalistic chittering that

reverberated throughout the enclosed space with ominous clarity. Scanning their surroundings, their flashlight beams moved from corner to corner in a vain attempt to locate the source of the unsettling noise. As the illumination moved along the floor and up the sides of the walls, the chittering increased in volume, growing even more frantic. Then, the beams of light reached the corners of the roof and they cried out in abject terror.

Stuck in the rafters was the body of a young man. Or, to be more precise, what had once been a body; it was torn to shreds, some of the tortured flesh plastered across the ceiling, but most of it just hanging over the struts like a butchered animal. This was the source of the smell, and, most likely, the source of the diagram's blood. More than that, it was the source of the horrific sound.

All along the ceiling, covering the rafters, and in every darkened crevice, swarmed huge, rat-like things. They'd been feeding in silence until the beams of light had interrupted their gruesome meal. Now they were enraged. Beady eyes glared out from folded, desiccated faces while razor sharp teeth gleamed from hundreds of screeching mouths. In a frightening wave of repugnance, the horde of creatures poured from their places of concealment, boiling down the walls and spreading out across the floor. Williams backpedaled toward the exit, dropping the flashlight as he pulled off a shot that slammed him through the jagged edge of the hole. Terry was squeezing off round after round, firing into the teeming multitudes as they came surging toward them, but the bullets seemed to have little effect.

Regaining his balance, Williams continued to fire as he staggered across the floor. Each time he sent a round into the pulsating wave of creatures, his arms were nearly wrenched from their sockets. Soon, he realized, he would run out of ammo. Knowing it was their only chance, he turned and pushed Terry out the attic door, following her and slamming it hard behind him. The door vibrated with the impact of the creatures as they pounded against the other side, chewing, clawing, and scrabbling at the ancient wood. Realizing the door wouldn't hold for long, he rushed Terry to the stairs and then bolted down them, heading for the lower levels.

It occurred to him that they were already running for their lives and hadn't even begun to uncover the answers that they'd come here to find. He glanced down at the pouch around his neck as they reached the second story landing. The Elder Sign was still vibrating, even more so as they neared the bottom of the stairwell. It was the only connection they had. Somehow, the bizarre relic was responding to whatever was going on in this godforsaken place. It was the key to all of it, he just knew it.

Pausing in the secluded darkness, he caught his breath as they reloaded their weapons. The look in each others' eyes was enough to convey their shared feelings of dread so he didn't bother trying to discuss what had happened. Then, as they collected themselves for a final dash down the remaining steps, he became aware of something just at the edges of their perception. Rising above the wind, the thunder, and the hellish fury of the scrabbling rat-like things, even above the echoes of their own harsh breathing, was a deep, reverberant chant. It was coming from somewhere far below, perhaps even from the hidden tunnels themselves.

On the floor above them, they heard the attic door give way in an explosion of splintering wood. Williams glanced toward the front door on the main floor below; there, he could see more of the foul creatures pouring in through the doorway, no doubt summoned by their brethren's maddened squealing.

Clasping the pouch around his neck, he felt the fear slowly recede as he was overcome by a sense of sudden clarity. He knew then what they needed to do. There could be no escape for them now. Instead, they must go down, deep into the bowels of the house. The answers they sought, and perhaps even their own salvation, could only be found at the source of that horrid, guttural chanting. Something was down there, something far more terrifying than he could even guess at, but that was where they must go in order to overcome this madness.

From somewhere within himself, he found the courage. Adjusting his glasses, he shouldered the shotgun as he studied Terry in the wane illumination of their remaining flashlight. She was pale, but her compressed lips and hooded eyes said it all; she had come to the same conclusions.

They would confront this unknown threat together and, God willing, they would put an end to it once and for all.

***

Candlelight flickered and danced in the age-old vault of sacrifice, reaching through the mist shrouded darkness to wash over the cloaked figure standing before the pitted altar. Back within the towering shadows, the hideous canine minions writhed and chanted, adding their combined power to the ongoing ritual. The figure, raising its arms toward the vaulted ceiling, called out in forgotten tongues, appealing to the beings beyond time and space, striving with arcane might to open a rift in the planes that would allow the mighty Nathrotep to descend from the heavens. Swirling throughout the air and joining their whispering voices to the cadence, swam the viperous, snake-like beings, their jet-black coils moving in intricate, hypnotic patterns. This time, there would be no girl sobbing in fear at the back of that unhallowed vault, for these were not the frightening dreams of some unsuspecting child.

Unlike the nightmares he'd been using to batter down his daughter's mental defenses, this was reality.

Ezekial P. Jedidiah, Grand Master of the Cult of the

Messenger, reveled in his newfound freedom. His ancestors had been drawn here over a hundred years ago, forming the cult around this ancient nexus of power. They had been ordered to open a gateway, a portal into the world of men and, in return, would be granted power beyond anything they'd ever imagined. So they had made an unbreakable pact; the undertaking would be built upon throughout the ages, to be passed down from generation to generation, until the gates of the monstrous cataract could be torn asunder.

And now that pact was about to be fulfilled.

It was only by the sheerest luck that Ezekial had had the chance to implant a portion of himself into the psyche of his daughter at the time of his death. And it had condemned him to an eleven year vigil embedded within the minds and deeds of others. His faithless wife had done this to him, and she would pay for it a thousand times over before this night was through. As Robin had lain on the altar stone watching him burn in agony so long ago, he'd buried himself within her, the initial splicing of their minds done quickly as the flames consumed him. She'd been the one being offered up that night, flesh of his flesh being the ultimate sacrifice, but his wife, Carol, had turned on him right before the dagger's plunge. In her moment of ultimate betrayal, she had destroyed him with a fiery candelabra and then whisked the child away to safety.

Deep in thought, Ezekial moved to kneel at the corner of the altar platform, a speculative frown creasing his girlish features as he dug through the pile of scorched remains that rested there. Invading the mind of the psychopath had been another fortuitous move on his part. It was by his will alone that Zak had been persuaded to kill his ex and then flee with the unborn child that fateful night. Mastering the sharing of spirit with his daughter at the same time as he was setting the compulsion within Zak to return had been difficult, but Ezekial had managed it all too well. Then, he had been forced to remain hidden within the folds of Robin's developing mind until his unsuspecting servant could be lured back to facilitate his release.

Fortunately, the Hunting Horrors had suffered a similar fate. They had visited many painful atrocities upon him during their time of mutual imprisonment, but they had soon come to realize that their only hope of freedom might lay within the actions of the madman. Because of this they had not refused Ezekial's command when he'd bidden them to seek Zak out. Their success in 'befriending' him, and showing him the ways of his newfound power, had been invaluable.

Grunting in satisfaction, he finally found what he was looking for amongst the soot covered bones that were all that remained of his other, once fleshy form. Settling back on slender haunches, he lifted the pulsating blade free, blowing the ash from its shimmering surface. Then, surging to his feet, he raised the knife on high. The thunderous response of the Children was tremendous, causing him to swell with self importance at their eager expectancy. With renewed purpose, he made his way back to the altar.

This night would be the culmination of all the Cult of the Messenger had planned from the start, an end to the ritual that had hung in the balance for over a century. Tonight he would summon the Mighty Messenger of the Outer Gods, the great Nathrotep. The words of power were his, as was the blade, the Hunting Horrors, and the teeming Children of the Graves. They would all lend their voices, adding more than enough power to his appeal. Tonight, the doors of the monstrous cataract would be flung wide, allowing the soul and herald of the mighty outer deities to come down from the stars to mock and rejoice at his humble, living sacrifice.

Raw energy coursed through him as he stared down at the struggling young woman chained to the pitted stone. That had been another result of his bold ingenuity; the summoning of his daughters closest friends. He'd known they would come, had gotten the information from the mind of the lad he'd used to transport Robin's unconscious body through the tunnels. And he had desperately needed those friends to seal his bargains with the other various minions now under his control. Bending over the whimpering girl, he shrugged away all further thoughts of the mortal realm. It was of no matter; soon the ritual would be complete, and Nathrotep would be free to prepare the world for the dominion of the elder gods.

None could hope to stop him now.

Reaching down, he ran one slim, feminine hand up the bare leg of the quivering sacrifice, moving along the inner thigh and thrilling to the feel of smooth, silky flesh beneath his own. Yes, she would make the perfect offering; so soft, so sweet. Surely the earth would tremble this night, and, as he marshaled himself for the powerful climax of the ancient spell, the maddened look in his eyes bespoke an ageless power.

-15-

The beam of the remaining flashlight cut a thin path through the shadows, painting the boxes and crates in a dim, yellow glow. Terry knew they'd been lucky enough to find the entrance to the basement right beneath the stairwell and, now that they were safe behind its heavy oaken timbers, she was breathing a little easier. It would be a good long time before anything could break through that stout barrier. But as they reached the bottom of the basement staircase, she was left wondering why they'd needed such an imposing door there in the first place.

Shrugging away the useless speculation, she focused on the task at hand. The chanting had stopped, fading away until it was no longer audible. The lack of it would make finding the tunnels more challenging, but her gut instinct told her that they would somehow uncover its hidden location. She only hoped that Williams could hold it together that long; he'd been acting strangely since they'd left the upper levels and it worried her.

"Doc?" she asked, "are you doing okay?"

"I'm fine," he replied, pushing his glasses up. "Let's just keep moving."

She narrowed her eyes as he strode past her. He wasn't fooling anyone; the shotgun was wavering in his hands and beads of sweat stood out on his forehead even in the cold, dank air. There was something going on with him, something that she couldn't quite put her finger on, and she really didn't know what to make of it. Shaking her head in annoyance, she continued forward without further comment.

There was a lot she'd learned about the supernatural in college, but what was going on here went far beyond her range of studies. She was beginning to think that they wouldn't be able to handle whatever they found beneath this accursed place. If the things they'd seen so far were any indication of what to expect, then they were in a lot of trouble. She prayed that the relics they'd gotten from Jarrod would give them some kind of an edge, but she couldn't begin to fathom what the strange items were meant for. The wand was obviously some kind of juju fetish, but the Elder Sign was still a complete mystery to her. The realization that she'd have to do whatever it took just to survive down here terrified her. Pushing the unsettling thoughts to the back of her mind, she followed Williams deeper into the darkness.

While the first chambers were little more than storage, they soon found themselves in a much larger room. Long sheets of spider silk flowed down from the ceiling arches and it was filled with endless piles of junk and bulky furniture. As they made their way across, she could tell that some of the objects had been recently shifted; the marks on the floor were quite apparent and many of the items were no longer coated in thick layers of dust. But it was Williams who first spotted the footprints.

"What do you make of these?" he asked, kneeling down to take a closer look.

"I don't know," she replied. "They look kinda like tennis shoes. I just don't—wait! Teenagers, maybe, judging by the size of them. Oh my God! What if there are more kids down here?"

Running his hand along the length of a print, he considered it a moment before turning back to reply. Then he paused, eyes going wide as they locked onto something just behind her. As she watched on in growing concern, all the color drained from his face.

Pivoting, she shined the light in the direction of his paralyzed stare. Not ten feet away stood a man shrouded in luminescent mist. A reddish glow suffused his filthy, bearded features, and his tattered, black robes were covered in layers of grime. As she gazed at him in surprise, he muttered something under his breath and then flung up both his arms, fists clenched tightly around a sudden storm of crackling energy. Snapping them back down, he uttered a single, sharp syllable, "Shokk!"

Yet even as the unclean power blazed forth in a repellent wave, a blast from the shotgun took him in the chest, throwing him back onto an antique table. It shattered under his weight and he went down in a cascade of blood and fizzling, unspent potency. Stunned by the backlash of the spell washing over them, Terry collapsed to the ground, choking on bile. The sensation was like a million tiny hands raking slimy fingernails across her skin, poking and prodding at her with hate-filled intent. If the malignant force would have hit them full on, she knew they'd be mindless husks by now, cowering and convulsing along the floor. It made her shudder all the more as she fought back against her ebbing tide of revulsion. As she struggled to regain control, she saw that Williams was still kneeling, the shotgun propped against his hip. Taking a long, steadying breath, he turned to her.

"You all right?" he asked.

"Y-Yes," she stammered. "I. . . I think so. That must be. . . must be one of the cultists. I think you got him before he could finish. . ."

At a loss for words, she rocked back and forth, trying desperately to rid herself of the unclean feelings. With what must have been a monumental effort on his part, Williams got to his feet, pulling her up beside him.

"From now on, we stick close together," he said. "I'll take the lead, but you stay right behind me, okay?"

"All right," she managed, bending to gather up the flashlight.

Pumping another round into the chamber, he advanced toward the spot where the cultist had fallen. Terry followed, still shaking as she tried to illuminate the spot for him in the light of the unsteady beam.

As they drew nearer, they almost gagged on the foul stench rising up from the crumpled pile. It was overpowering, permeating the air with nauseating strength. Kicking aside an old chair that was in his path, Williams gazed down at the reeking corpse. It was beyond grotesque, sprawled out across the floor with one leg held upright by a piece of broken table and the other one bent back at an unnatural angle. A thin curl of smoke rose in a lazy spiral from the hole in the center of its chest. It was not a pretty sight. Without studying it further, they backed away in disgust, then worked themselves around the tangle of furniture to continue on their way beyond it. In the direction from which the cultist had appeared, all they could see was more useless junk extending back to the far wall.

"Are you sure he's dead?" Terry asked in a small voice.

"I'm sure," he stated quietly.

"Well," she replied, clearing her throat, "over there, toward the back of the room; that's where he must have come from—"

"Terry," he cut in, "take the spool of twine out of my pack."

"What? Why?"

"Just do it! We need something to secure that flashlight; I don't like the way we seem to keep dropping it."

"Okay, okay, I got it," she flared. "You know, it's not easy keeping the gun steady and holding the flashlight at the same time! Especially with this wand taped to it!"

Tucking the sidearm into her belt, she proceeded to fish out the twine, and then cut off a long piece of it with her pocketknife. The momentary burst of anger faded as she worked, leaving her feeling contrite and somewhat ashamed.

"I'm sorry—it's just this place; it's really getting to me," she told him. Then, as the reality of what had just happened started to sink in, she blurted, "What if. . . what if we don't make it? What if. . . oh, what the hell are we even doing here? Maybe we should have just called the police and let them handle it."

Turning, he gripped her by the shoulder, shaking it a little. "We've got to find out what's going on here and put an end to it," he said, "You know that the cops would never believe us if we told them. And even if we did somehow get them to come down here, it'd all be over before we got back. I can feel the artifact pulsing at my neck—it's reacting to whatever's happening in those tunnels and it wants us to go down there. Besides, we'd have to fight our way back past all those things upstairs if we left now. Our only chance to get out of this alive is to follow it through to the end."

As he let that hang in the air, Terry realized that he was right. He was babbling a bit, but all-in-all he was correct. They had to go on, had to at least try to break up whatever ritual was being performed. Perhaps the tunnels themselves would lead them to another exit; there had to be more than one way out of this place. Kneeling briefly, she tied the flashlight's utility loop to her wrist. Now, in case of any other surprises, it would dangle there, ready to be swung back up into her hand. He watched her, pupils round in the uncertain light.

Nodding to show that she was ready, she followed him as he headed toward the back of the room. While moving through the piles of random junk, she noticed that a lot of the larger objects were set up in a crude sort of maze. It made her think of the footprints they'd found, and of the young man hanging in pieces above them in the attic. Shuddering, she hoped that whomever had set up this maze hadn't suffered a similar fate. The thought was still troubling her as they approached the far wall. Upon reaching it, they found nothing but a pile of stacked saw horses, a few bolts of rotted cloth, and an antique wardrobe.

Placing a finger to his lips, Williams nodded toward the wardrobe, and Terry could see that its door was slightly ajar. Before she could speak, Williams pointed to the door, then to himself, motioning for her to back away and cover him. He waited for her to get into position, then kicked the door hard over on rusty hinges.

Terry screamed as something fell on her from above, causing her to career backward into some crates as its cold, wet arms wrapped tightly around her. Thrashing about, furniture and other items came crashing down as she fought against the unknown assailant. Williams jumped forward, attempting to see what was happening, but the flashlight spun on its new tether, sending fluttering shadows flickering all around them. In helpless frustration, he knelt and grabbed at the substance that entangled her face and arms. It felt horrid, like the slimy strands of a decaying jellyfish. Releasing the disgusting tendrils, he instead grabbed the flashlight from out of mid-air as it whizzed past him, shining its light fully upon her.

Then he burst out laughing.

Terry was so shocked, she stopped her fearful thrashing. Peering down, she saw that she was covered in what appeared to be clothesline tied into a web. It was doused with something purple and wet, like the gooey stuff she'd seen on Saturday morning television, and it had fake bugs tied all through it.

"There was someone else in here all right," Williams chuckled, directing the light into the closet to reveal a shelf containing a 1954 license plate. A smirk was twitching at the corners of his mouth as he glanced up. "Looks like it was rigged to fall from the ceiling."

She glared at him in mock indignation, then exploded into a fit of nervous giggling. Grinning, he assisted her to her feet, untangling the man-made web and throwing it to the floor. So great was her relief that she felt giddy and then quite foolish.

"Well, they sure pulled one over on us," she said, wiping a tear from the corner of her eye. "Ugh! It's all in my hair! I must look terrible."

"You never look terrible," he replied with sincerity.

She paused a moment, transfixed by his penetrating stare. Gazing back into the depths of his eyes, she realized that there was something there, something warm and utterly surprising, and she was amazed to find herself responding to it. As she was taking stock of this newfound emotion, he reached up and gently brushed a strand of purple slime from her cheek.

"You know, you look good in purple," he murmured.

Before she could formulate a cohesive response, the wardrobe jolted forward, smashing into them and forcing them apart. Her cries reverberated throughout the room as something small and yammering flew out of the darkness to attach itself to her face.

Shoving the wardrobe out of the way, Williams leapt past it with no thought for his own safety. The thing on her head was an evil blur of thrashing limbs and biting teeth, filling the air with high-pitched squeaks and mewling sounds. Growling like a madman, he swung the butt of the shotgun around, trying to knock it away from her, but before the blow could even connect, he was yanked backward off his feet. The shotgun clattered to the floor as he grasped at the sinewy fingers now digging into his windpipe.

"Zaaaa. . . kkkk. . . "

The harsh, rasping statement was like a thunderclap

above the noise of the struggle. With all her might, Terry battled her attacker as Williams was pulled back and pinioned against the wall. Adrenalized by fear and incredible pain, Terry flailed at the small creature, but still could not seem to rid herself of the horrible thing. She could hear Williams wailing over her own cries as she felt herself spiraling ever closer to the edges of madness.

"Barbara, my love!" A chilling voice suddenly called out from the darkness. "What a fine catch you have there. And, my son! What a good boy you are to help us subdue that nasty lady. . ."

Heaving in further panic, Terry caught sight of the speaker. She could barely believe her eyes, but there was no doubt that this was the cultist that they'd just shot. While struggling to free herself from the child-thing's brutal attack, she could see him outlined in the reddish glow surrounding his hellish body. He was oozing blood, but otherwise seemed very much alive.

"So!" the man crowed, "you have now met my family! Aren't they wonderful? Barbara, where are your manners? Give the young gentleman a kiss! He is our very special guest this evening. And, by the way, dear—then rip his fucking head off!"

As the bony hands of the creature flipped Williams around, Terry caught a glimpse of it while she continued to fight the thing that was still tearing away at her. It was the corpse of a young woman, far gone in decay. With brutal strength, its skeletal hands pulled Williams into a repulsive embrace, rotted lips pressing tightly against his own. Retching, he fell back against the wall as it then seized him by the neck and began to twist. He was no longer even attempting to fight back.

Witnessing that, Terry's vision clouded over in a red haze. Something inside of her snapped, and she was overcome by white-hot rage.

The handgun came up from her belt, and she blasted the yammering demon child from her face in a splatter of rotted debris. Surging up from the broken furniture, she got one knee under her, and then planted three more rounds into the cultist without even aiming. The high caliber bullets tore him in half as he flew backward into some crates. Without pausing, she pivoted, emptying the rest of the clip into the creature that was holding Williams by the neck. He slid farther down the wall as the thing's head exploded, showering him with thick, greenish-brown slime.

"That will be quite enough of that, I think," Terry said, breathing hard as she got her feet under her and then staggered over to Williams.

"Flashlight. . . check to see. . . " he gasped, wobbling a bit as she helped him to stand upright.

Flipping the swinging light back into her hand, she scanned their surroundings.

"Yep," she observed. "I got 'em, Doc. I . . . I killed them all. . . "

Slumping back against the wall, they slid to the ground together, huddling in shock as she continued to shine the light around them in trembling, irregular arcs. As the beam flashed across the chipped plaster of the wall next to them, she brought it to an unsteady halt—there was a hole where the wardrobe had been. A large hole.

It had to be the entrance they'd been searching for.

"Oh, joy—we've found the tunnels," Williams rasped before falling into a strained silence. Then, the silence crumbled as the diabolical chanting starting up once more. This time, it hammered up at them from the depths of the earth, relentless as the waves of a storm-tossed sea.

-16-

The vaulted chamber pulsed and echoed with Ezekial's vibrant voice, the strange words bursting forth from the full lips of the body he now controlled while the Children responded to the chant in their own guttural tongue. Sweat poured off him as a vortex began to form, catching the dim light of the candles and collecting it in its dense, all-consuming grasp. With every fiber of his being, he strained to push the powerful chant even further out across the multitudinous dimensions, seeking celestial lifeforms that were never meant for the eyes of man to see.

And they began to respond.

With greater confidence, he poured his mastery into the ancient spell, seeking, compelling, demanding that they submit to his will. His power was vast, yet greater still was the strength of the beings that replied, and his mind soon rang with the vibrations of their chaotic thoughts. Yet he reveled in it. This was his chance to commune with the Old Ones, to gain the power he'd longed for, and to achieve his dreams of immortality. He would exist forever within the embrace of living death, giving into the places between while his dark influence enfolded the world within its unyielding grasp.

He would be a god!

As he completed the last segment of the complex spell, he fell to his knees in front of the altar, lifting his soft, feminine hands in supplication. Swirling in the air was now the start of an astral portal, pulsating like a giant blue-and-white whirlpool of lightning-streaked clouds. It was more than half complete; a few more passages of the vile chant and he'd be able to make the sacrifice, summoning the great Nathrotep into the realm of men. It was the moment that he'd been preparing for his entire life.

Kneeling in the midst of the churning, snake-like Horrors, he reached out, running a hand along the rough, eel-like skin of one as it slid past, then giggled in morbid delight. The thing hissed, resenting his touch as it wriggled away through the roiling mists. Then, still chuckling, he climbed to his feet, preparing himself for the final segment of the ancient ritual. His new rapport with the creatures beyond the gate allowed him to draw from their blinding energy, much like a piglet would suckle its mother's teat, and he knew this added power would soon be needed if he were going to tear a hole in the very fabric of time and space itself. With their tremendous energy coursing through him, he glanced down, his face shining with glorious intensity.

The girl was no longer screaming; she now lay panting and glassy-eyed, her nakedness gleaming snow-white in the glow of the incomplete gateway. What a fine sacrifice she'll make! he thought, pulling the shimmering dagger from the sash of his robe. Soon, very soon indeed, it would be time. Oh, how the world would tremble at his greatness then, and taste the extent of his terrible power! As the key disciple of the Old Ones, he would destroy any and all that got in his way! He would. . .

Something in the back of his mind briefly pulled at his attention; a link that he'd forged within another's consciousness being irrevocably severed. Startled, his concentration wavered for just a brief moment.

That was all it took.

The Hunting Horrors swarmed in, lashing out with

razor-sharp claws and tearing at him with vicious, jagged-edged teeth. In a dozen places he was bloodied before he could regain control. Then, reasserting his will, he struck back with all the power he'd milked from the nebulous outer entities. Lightning flared within in the chamber, cascading around the flying shapes with sudden ferocity. In their present state of being, they sizzled in the electrified air, twisting away from him as their blunted, irregular snouts screeched out in futile rage.

Torrents of energy coursing through him revealed what he'd already surmised; the madman and his family had failed.

A slow smirk of utter contempt crept across his features as he lashed out at the Horrors again, watching as they howled in indescribable pain. They would regret defying him; he was not a man to be trifled with, oh no, not at all! He was the high priest of the mighty Nathrotep, and his will was absolute! Aside from the momentary distraction, Zak's failure was of no real concern; the trespassers would soon be taken care of by the Children gathering in the sacred entrance hall. With hardly a thought, he sent a tendril of his newly acquired power out to command the lesser beings that congregated there.

They would stop this meddlesome couple before they got any closer with that accursed relic. And even if they somehow failed, the dweller in the sunken catacombs would surely see to it that they advanced no further. Not even the Children were willing to linger in those benighted chambers. None could hope to stop him now.

His oath-bound minions would take care of everything.

-17-

Many of Terry's wounds were superficial, but there was one cut just above her right eye that kept weeping blood. With the backward swipe of a hand, she smeared it away, gasping at the fresh pain that exploded across her brow. It probably needed stitches, but there was nothing she could do about it now. Besides, the rest of her wasn't in much better shape; countless bites and scratches throbbed in the dank air of the passageway as they moved downward.

It had taken her quite some time to convince Williams to enter the tunnels; he was badly shaken, the horror of what they'd experienced having worn away at his courage bit by bit. In the semi-darkness, she could see the fear written plainly across his pale features. He'd lost his glasses during the scuffle, and his tousled hair now seemed to have taken on quite a few new streaks of gray. She knew he wouldn't be able to hold up much longer unless she found a way to refocus his slipping resolve. It would be difficult, but she couldn't give up on him; he was depending on her, and she planned to see him through this thing to the end, no matter what the cost.

Still, she did not like the odds.

They'd been traveling for a while now, making their way down a large, mist-filled corridor. The noisome walls were covered in a series of curling, intricate patterns that confused the eye, and about every ten feet or so was a niche filled with the remains of some long-forgotten soul. Many of the bones had been disturbed and it looked to her as if they'd also been gnawed on. Swallowing heavily, she wiped the back of a hand across her eyes again to clear away the blood.

"Doc?" she whispered. "I don't hear the chanting anymore, do you?"

Stopping, he fiddled with the shotgun as he muttered back over his shoulder, "No, I don't hear it either. . ." Then he retreated a step. "Maybe we should return to the basement. . ."

Placing her hand on the small of his back, she applied a firm yet gentle pressure, urging him along.

"You know we have to do this," she cajoled. "Think of Robin; if we don't succeed, she may not even survive. We have to finish this now, before it's too late. Barnaby. . . remember your father."

It was a cruel thing to say, and it pained her to say it, but it had the desired effect. Grunting like he'd been kicked in the stomach, he straightened his shoulders, then continued to follow the darkened pathway.

"You're right, and I'm sorry," he said after a moment, his voice raw with emotion. "It's just this place! I don't know if I can take much more of this; the walls are closing in on me, and I hear voices."

"What kind of voices?" she asked.

"You don't want to know," he replied with finality.

Although she listened for the next few minutes, she could hear nothing but the scuffle of their feet and the harshness of their own breathing. With a feeling of uncertainty, she chose to ignore the comment.

As the tunnel widened out, the intricate designs receded back into patterns that began to glow with their own unexpected light. It came from the walls themselves, climbing in and around the designs in a hypnotically disturbing way. Soon, they could see each other clearly in the pasty-green glow.

"It's the lichens."

"What?" she asked, startled.

"The lichens and mosses," he said, "they're bio-luminescent. I read about it somewhere."

With dreadful reluctance, she let her eyes focus on the menacing hieroglyphics. They swam in and out of her vision like gigantic worms struggling against one another in an effort to hold up the ceiling. In quivering revulsion, she turned her face away, burying it in the folds of his shirt.

"Make them stop!" she cried out, her face smothered by material.

Pausing, Williams encircled her waist with his free arm.

"Don't worry, Terry," he whispered into her silken hair. "These designs can't hurt you, and they're actually kind of beautiful in a way."

Leaning back from him, she stared into his burning eyes. He was further gone than she'd thought. With a concentrated effort, she pulled herself together.

"You're right," she said. "They can't hurt us and they're really quite helpful. I can see much better now. Let's just keep moving; we need to find out what's at the end of this tunnel."

As they continued onward, the going got easier with the increased visibility. Soon they began to notice smaller tunnels burrowed right into the central corridor. There was a crude, rough-hewn look about them, like the ones made by animals. Stooping, Williams studied one of the many openings, his head tilted to the side.

"These seem to branch off in all directions," he observed. "But I think it's best that we continue along this main route for now. I just don't know if—"

"What's that?" she cut in.

"What?" he asked, glancing around.

"Shhhh! Listen!"

Faint echoes came to them from out of the depths. A

low, throaty sound, cruel and gravelly, interspersed with a guttural, choppy-sounding barks, like that of a small dog. She couldn't quite place it—it was like nothing she'd ever heard before. She was already frightened, but this was affecting her on a deeper level. The sounds were so. . . inhuman. And, much more than that, so unsettling that they called up the memories of childhood demons that had plagued her sleep so long ago. Shrinking back, she grasped Williams by the arm.

"You hear it now too, don't you?" she whispered.

"Y-Yes. . ." he responded in a voice dulled by fear.

She was not at all surprised to find him trembling. This place was taking its dark toll on both of them and she didn't even want to think about what might lay ahead. It was enough that they just kept pressing forward as best they could.

For better or for worse.

The sounds became clearer as they crept closer, sending fresh thrills of uncertainty down her spine. Up ahead, the tunnel rounded a bend, the luminescent patterns growing brighter as the unholy grunts and harsh braying became more distinct. Whatever was lying around that bend, whatever horrors awaited just beyond that fateful turn, she couldn't even guess at, but no single animal could make such a cacophony of unnatural noise. There had to be a group of creatures to make that much steady clamor.

Or so she feared.

Rounding the corner, they braced themselves for whatever they'd find, but it didn't prepare them for the truth of their discovery. Recoiling in shock, they almost fled in panic before being caught up by the monstrous spectacle.

They were on a small ledge overlooking a cave. Seething masses of bio-luminescent growths covered the entire chamber, and the floor was dotted with sulfurous pools of bubbling liquid. But that was not the source of the unwholesome noise, nor the cause of their almost insurmountable terror. Back within the shadows, not more than fifty feet from where they stood, was a gathering of loathsome creatures.

They were humanoid in shape, their spindly, bipedal forms surging back and forth as they grunted and barked in their incomprehensible tongue. But that's where the similarities to humanity ended. Their angular, misshapen bodies displayed awkward movements, as if their joints were in all the wrong places, while their features were distinctly canine, with softly glowing eyes and sharp, jagged teeth. They were so intent upon whatever it was they were doing, that they had yet to notice the frightened couple standing rigid in the shadows above them.

Terry swallowed her rising fear and disgust, trying to become detached enough to study the scene objectively, but looking over at Williams, she noted that he didn't seem to be handling it very well. Deciding that a retreat would be the best option for now, she motioned him back around the corner, sparing a glance down at the boiling mass of deformed beasts as they moved away. The creatures were fighting each other in an attempt to get at the middle of their gathering, and it was there that she caught a glimpse of more vigorous movements—perhaps some kind of pulsating dance or other ritualistic behavior. It made her wonder, in morbid fascination, just what the creatures were doing in the center of that hellish mob.

Retracing their steps, they rounded the bend and Williams released an explosive breath as he slid down the wall, cradling the shotgun across his knees.

"D-did y-y-you see it?" he finally stuttered.

"Yes, those. . . things. . . whatever they are, are doing something in the middle of that cave, something horrible!"

"No!" he cried hoarsely. "On the far side of that. The doorway—the one we must go through if we are to continue."

"You mean you don't think they're the cause of everything that's been happening?"

Sighing, he ran a trembling hand through his disheveled hair. "No. They're animals! Perverted, malformed creatures! Can't you hear them?" He thrust out his arm, wagging a finger toward the guttural barking. "The chanting we heard earlier, the ritualistic voice that came from somewhere far below us, could not possibly have been made by that group of. . . of twisted abominations!"

She was amazed by his vehemence but also impressed at his reasoning. The gathering of creatures had held her attention in such a way that she'd thought of little else. "I think you're right," she conceded. "I guess I was so caught up by the sight of them that I just wasn't thinking. What the hell are those things anyway? And what are they even doing down there?"

"I don't know. Maybe they're the things that Jarrod spoke of, or maybe they're some kind of guardians—I just don't know! But I do know this; the path we must follow lies just beyond them. I can feel the Elder Sign pulling me in that direction, can feel its hunger, its appetite. We have to go through them, and we have to do it now, before it's too late. Before I lose what little courage I have left. . ."

She stared at him. He was a pale shadow of his former self and she felt a great surge of compassion for the man that he once had been. He'd been so gentle, never overbearing or rude—always the perfect gentleman. And his home life, before he'd run away, it had all been so hard on him. She'd often wondered why he was single and now she could fathom the struggle that had been going on inside him. It was a one-sided battle to escape the blanket of shame his father had wrapped him in, to prove to himself that he was not a coward, that he was indeed a man. And look where it had led him. Truly he was the bravest person she'd ever known, and, she realized in wonder, she loved him for it.

Now, he was slipping away little by little, and she had brought him to this; it was at her insistence that they'd pursued this matter. No, that wasn't quite fair, not to her, nor to him. He had wanted to do something about the situation —she'd just helped him to decide, inspired him to be the man she'd always known him to be. Now, she needed to support him or they'd both die here in this godforsaken place.

Ignoring the malicious hooting of the barbarous creatures, she cupped her hand beneath his chin, lifting it up so she could catch his eyes.

"We'll get through this, Doc. I know we will. But we have to be strong now. Let's just get in there and do some damage; there can't be more than thirty of them. As long as we go in shooting and keep a level head, we can beat them. Just remember, whatever happens, I care about you. When this is all over, we're going to have a nice long chat, just the two of us. I promise."

With a lopsided grin, he stood and readied his weapon, shaking off his fear with a determined look in his eyes. Then, driving themselves forward, they rounded the corner and reached the overhang together. Williams immediately jumped down, then braced himself and began firing into the crowd of malformed beasts. Terry simply crouched on the ledge and started methodically picking off the creatures one by one. The effect of their weapons was devastating, but also unexpected; after felling about twenty of the beings, a greater amount of them came pouring in through the side tunnels that pocketed the walls.

There were hundreds of them, barking and clambering over one another in a surging mass of death itself. It was as if they were a single, gargantuan creature, wave upon wave of grotesque, pinkish flesh boiling forward in a screeching tide that threatened to wash away their very existence. Terry screamed once before her voice failed her. Williams just kept on firing.

Sinking forward onto her hands and knees, she swayed as she stared out over the advancing horde. Her movements were sluggish, like she was floating through thickened honey, and below her she could see Williams pulling off his last couple of shots and then struggling to reload. As she toppled forward, the beam of her flashlight flickered off the faces of the advancing nightmare, glinting in their cloudy, inhuman eyes, playing off the moist, slime-covered walls and unclean bodies, whirling around as she hit the floor and rolled. The last thing she knew before the blackness finally claimed her was a strange keening sound in the air above her.

-18-

Williams saw Terry fall as the gibbering pack surged toward him. There was nothing he could do; the shotgun was resisting his feverish attempts at reloading, and the things were almost upon him, their cadaverous pink flesh glinting in the fungal illumination. Their blunt-nosed snouts, filled with razor-sharp fangs, were looming so close now that he could see the splintery, red veins standing out in their glowing white eyes. Throwing his back against the cold, lichen-covered wall, he managed to jack a single round into the chamber before dropping the rest of the shells in panic. Then, leveling the gun, he shouted into the face of his onrushing doom.

"Terry!"

He punctuated his lingering scream with a shot that blasted the head off the lead creature, sending it reeling into the onrushing tide of its feral companions. They cringed back with hisses of rage, and then, much to his continued horror, stopped to devour their fallen comrade while still others leapt forward. Grasping the gun by the barrel, tears sprang up in his eyes as he stood protectively over Terry. He would use the weapon as a crude club; none of these foul creatures would touch her as long as he was yet alive! But there were so many of them! He knew his chances were slim as he glared at the howling cluster of demons, but he would fight them all, fight them to the very brinks of Hell itself!

His laughter rang out in the chamber as he waded forward into the mob, swinging the shotgun in huge, bone-crushing arcs.

Then a blast of energy threw him to the ground. As he slammed into the rocky floor, the air was driven from his lungs and his eyes were instantly drawn to Jarrod's detestable-looking wand. It flared with power, a putrescent glow pulsing from the obscene foot that was fastened to its end. The murmuring creatures fell back before its sullen radiance, unsure of themselves, and this proved to be their undoing; the energy lashed out, catching them all in its crackling embrace. The screaming that arose as they burned was such an eruption of hellish sound that it brought a grim smile to Williams' battered face. Then, those few that survived, poured off through the darkened tunnels, seeking their escape. The destruction had been so great that there were piles of twisted corpses littering the floor all around him, the sheer magnitude of scorched bodies making him laugh in crazed disbelief.

Struggling to his knees, he moved to cradle Terry's head in his lap. The light of the wand was slowly fading, but its soft glow still reflected off her bruised and bloodied features. Cursing himself for a fool, he ripped strips of cloth from his shirt and cleaned away the blood and grime before binding her forehead with a makeshift bandage. It was the best that he could do for now. Weeping uncontrollably, he moaned over and over in a low voice as he sat rocking back and forth. His stupidity had led them to this; he should have known to bandage her wounds long ago. Now, the loss of blood and rigors of their horrendous task had taken their toll. It was a miracle that she was even still alive.

He sat that way for a time, keening into the empty spaces of the cavern while the smoke of the burning dead rose all around him.

-19-

Loathsome creatures leaped and gibbered as they chased Terry through glowing, rune-encrusted tunnels. With her heart pounding and her throat full of dust, she fled down the ancient corridors, but the filthy creatures loped along just behind her, their milky eyes burning as they barked out their hungry desires. She knew she must keep running or suffer a fate worse than death, yet the warren was an endless maze that offered her no escape.

The tunnel twisted in on itself, spinning around, and she was caught like a leaf on the wind, spiraling in dizzying circles as she flew across a foreign sky lit by unknown stars.

As she clawed her way up from the depths of the nightmare, she could hear a high-pitched moaning in the air above her. With a small cry, she slapped at the scaly hand caressing her cheek, shrinking away from its sickening touch. But it was no use; she was too sluggish, too addled by fear to put much force behind the blows. She tried to roll away, but then realized there was someone speaking to her.

The words were rough and blurry, at once familiar, yet somehow strange. As recognition blossomed within her fractured mind she ceased her feeble struggling.

So they weren't dead after all.

Williams was trying to sound reassuring, but the effect was ruined by the hoarseness of his voice. Relaxing into his embrace, she decided she didn't want to open her eyes just yet. After the horrible events of the last few hours it was a relief just to rest for a moment.

However, it wasn't much of a reprieve; she could still feel the cuts and bruises that throbbed across her entire body. As she drew in a deep, steadying breath, her senses were filled with the smells of rotten vegetation, gun powder, and the lingering stench of burning flesh. It broke the spell of her lethargy and she snapped fully awake, cracking her eyelids open to peer cautiously around.

Williams was leaning over her, cradling her head in his lap.

"W-what happened?" she mumbled.

He gazed down at her, his eyes haunted by the shadows of doubt.

"The wand," he finally replied. "It. . . did something to them. Before that. . . well, I think you must have fainted."

With a groan, she pushed herself up, scanning their surroundings. The moss and lichens had been somehow blackened and there were a great deal of smoking carcasses laying in piles all around her. The sight of so much carnage sickened her, as did the disgusting slime of the mushrooms that she'd crushed beneath her. The odorous pulp clung to her clothing, resisting her halfhearted attempts to wipe it away. Wincing, she reached for her pack and dragged it over. Her throat felt dryer than desert sand and her stomach was roiling with nausea.

Taking out a bottle of water, she opened it before raising it to her lips to take a long swallow. Then, she slid away from Williams, attempting to draw the tatters of her scattered intellect together enough to function. He watched, his features twisted in confusion, as she picked up her gun and ejected the clip with trembling hands.

"How long was I unconscious?" she asked, digging around in the pack for a box of ammo.

"I-I'm not sure—about two or three minutes I'd guess."

The quaver in his voice caught her by surprise, and she turned to study him. He was staring at her as if she'd just sprouted a third eye.

"What?" she demanded.

With a shaking hand, he reached out to stop her from loading the clip. "It's my fault—I should have been paying better attention."

Puzzled, she tilted her head to one side. "What do you mean?"

He gestured at her head. "Your wounds! You might have bled to death, and it's all my fault. I should have been more focused, more aware of what was going on around me. When you fell from the ledge, I didn't even know what to do —I just attacked those creatures and tried to keep them off you. But after the wand's energy had consumed them, all I could think of was how badly you'd been hurt. I should have done something for you earlier, helped you before you'd lost so much blood. . ."

As she listened to his anguished confession, her free hand moved to explore the ragged bandage tied around her forehead. It was sloppily done and caked with blood, but she felt her heart swell with compassion.

"Barnaby," she said gently. "Don't. Don't take this all onto yourself. I wasn't thinking about my wounds either, at least not in any rational way. This place, it's affecting us both. If you have to blame someone, then blame me; I was the one who convinced you to come here. But this ritual, these creatures—I think we're in way over our heads now. Maybe we should try to get out of here before it's too late. Is that thing around your neck still pulling at you?"

"Yes," he answered, "but you're not to blame for any of this; the responsibility was mine to begin with. You just helped me to realize its importance. Those creatures—I wasn't expecting there to be so many of them. As it stands now, we don't even know what else we might find down here. And yet the stone, it is still affecting me—it's a part of me now, like the beating of my heart. It wants me to move forward, but you're right; we should probably try and find a way out instead. It's just that. . . I feel like I'm losing my mind! It's like I'm being pulled in two directions at once!"

She found herself reaching out to squeeze his shoulder in acknowledgment of all he was going through. There was nothing more that she could do for him now; they'd just have to find a way back to the surface and deal with it then. She finished loading the clip, slammed it back in the gun, and then flipped the flashlight back up into her other hand as she climbed shakily to her feet. For a moment, she swayed with dizziness, but then shook it from her head like a dog shedding water. The unwelcome movement caused more pain, but it also snapped her senses back into sharper focus.

"Let's get going," she said, shouldering her pack and then tucking the gun into her waistband. "I don't want to wait around here for those things to regain their courage."

Nodding in agreement, he gathered up the fallen shotgun shells, jacking them into the chamber one at a time. After he'd finished loading and then gathered up his pack, they picked their way down the scorched, body-strewn incline, heading toward a large archway that awaited them at the other side of the cavern. She hoped it would lead to a way out; the side tunnels were probably choked with hideous creatures just waiting to pounce. As they crossed the chamber, she shined the light ahead of them, and was caught off guard when she saw what was resting on the ground where the creatures had been congregating. Its paleness stood out in stark contrast to the blackened surroundings.

As they reached the spot where it lay, they were totally unprepared for what they found.

It was the nude body of a young woman sprawled face down over a large rock. Her entire back was covered in oozing sores and liberally coated with a yellowish slime. On closer inspection, they found that the tortured flesh was the result of many small nips and bite marks, as if the beasts had been playful in their attentions.

"My God," Williams exclaimed, edging around the boulder to get a better look at her face. It was also covered in slime, one sightless eye gazing up through a tangle of long, black hair. Grunting as if he'd been punched, he sank to his knees, head bowed as if in silent prayer. After a moment, he pointed to something near the girl's head.

"Get a look at this," he said.

Swallowing her revulsion, Terry moved around the boulder, peering down at the spot he was indicating.

In the flashlight's beam, she could see that the girl's left hand was clutching something. It appeared to be a gold chain. Williams reached down to pry it from her fist, but flinched back as a low, gurgling moan suddenly burst from her battered throat.

Shocked that she was still alive, they bent forward to help, brushing the hair back from the terrible carnage of her swollen features. But they were too late. As they gazed on in helpless solicitude, her eyes clouded over and she wheezed out her final breath.

It was a surprise that she'd even lasted this long; her jaw was broken, hanging down at an unnatural angle, and more of the foul slime drooled continually from her shattered mouth. Williams turned his head away, swallowing hard to keep from retching.

With a heavy numbness inside, Terry let the hair fall back, covering the ruined face and hiding the sight of the sickening puddle spreading out across the stone. It took her a moment to regain her composure; it was the most grotesque thing she'd ever witnessed.

Sinking to the ground, she hugged herself while rocking back and forth. She now realized why the creatures had been so eager to get at the center of their gathering; they'd been rutting, pushed into a frenzy over this poor, hapless child. Like a piece of meat, they'd used her, feeding off her vitality as they brutalized her over and over. Terry knew how she must have felt, remembering the traumatic events of her adolescent years. Although she hadn't been treated in anywhere near as violent a fashion, she could well understand the pain and helplessness that the girl must have experienced.

Terry had been ten years old when her mother had remarried, and her stepfather and uncle had been insufferable. They'd abused her, off-and-on, until she was fourteen. That's when her mother had finally caught on and put an end to their 'little game'. It's what they'd called it, and, to a confused young girl who'd always trusted her elders, that's all it had been.

At first.

But by the time her mother had stopped the abuse, the damage had already been done. She'd never told anyone else about it, instead suffering from a deep, burning shame, and an ongoing belief that she'd somehow been sullied by all the things that they'd done to her. It was only after a long period of time that she'd come to grips with it, and even now it still affected her deeply.

Inside her, a raw-edged anger was building. The senseless mistreatment of this young woman had burst apart the walls she'd built within herself to hold back the unbearable memories. Now, all the intense shame and humiliation, all the impotent rage that she'd spent so much time walling away, boiled to the surface. She suddenly longed for justice, thirsted for it, not only for this unknown young woman, but for herself as well.

She was going to destroy the creatures who'd done this, and kill anything else that got in her way!

Panting like she'd just ran a marathon, she lurched to

her feet. Williams was still kneeling, cradling something in his open palm. Glancing at her through tear-blurred eyes, he held it up for her to see.

It was a golden locket. From inside, a picture of a man smiled out at her, his deep brown eyes staring up at her from a handsomely bearded face. Her boyfriend, perhaps.

"She. . . she was clutching that in her hand," he choked out, climbing to his feet. Then, with a look of utter hatred, he snarled, "We've got to burn this entire place down and rip it from the face of the earth! These brutal deaths, this sickening debauchery, we have to put an end to it. We can't allow it to continue!"

Snatching up the shotgun, he hefted it, the muscles of his neck and arms knotting up while the veins in his forehead throbbed visibly. "We may not make it out of this alive," he growled, "but we have to at least try and stop this madness. I know I've sometimes been afraid, that I may even be a coward at heart, but I swear to God that I'm going to wipe these bastards out, even if it kills me!"

Staring at him, gazing into those determined, red-rimmed eyes, she could see the blistering anguish, feel the terrible, white-hot fury that so closely mirrored her own. This was a different side to the man she thought she knew. Where she'd been so sure he'd lose control, he'd become more determined than ever. But this night wasn't over yet—they still had to stop the ritual, no matter what the cost.

Drawing courage from their mutual outrage, they turned toward the gigantic stone doors that barred their way forward. Just as they were studying the carved designs and the arcane sigils engraved along its marble facings, a low, throaty rumble burst over them. The diabolical chant had begun anew, its booming cadence rolling over them like the waves of the sea. This time, however, the effect was muted by their burning need for justice.

***

Power.

Deep, colossal, all-encompassing power. It coursed through Ezra like a thunderous wave, pouring through him as he recited the archaic words of the ancient chant. The passages of the ritual rebounded off the walls and ceiling of the chamber, echoing in and out of space and time with the forcefulness of a hurricane. He was mad with it, drunk with it, and so focused on finishing the complex spell that only his lips moved as he peered across the insubstantial barriers now breached by the astral gate.

The ritual was coming to an end, and Nathrotep was descending.

Now within reach of his triumphant success, he was completely unaware that the energy would consume him if he wavered for even a fraction of a second. Behind him, his oath-bound minions barked out a guttural cadence in time with his own thunderous voice, lending him the strength of their life force. But that extra power was no longer needed; he could finish the working all on his own, for he was that powerful and knew it. The Hunting Horrors went unnoticed as they swarmed through the air, and the Children covering the floor behind him had also faded from his conscious thoughts. The entire chamber had so receded from his current level of perception that even the young woman chained to the altar stone before him was, for the time being, not one of his immediate concerns. The power was his, the spell all but finished; all else was beneath him.

It was thus that he failed to notice a portion of the wall sliding inward, exposing a dark niche just to the left of the altar. Deep within it, a shrouded presence lingered. It neither moved nor tried to interfere; it simply watched, cloaked from head to toe in the dark colors of the grave.

-20-

The chant vibrated outward from beyond the door, the unclean phrases washing over them with rhythmic force as Williams glared at the huge portal with barely suppressed rage. He felt like he'd been pushed around his whole life, living in constant fear of failure while trying to carve out a place for himself where he could make a difference. That was one of the reasons that he'd taken a job in this small, out-of-the-way town; no one there had known him and he'd been able to make a fresh start of it.

But now the things he'd seen and the decisions he'd made had landed him in the toughest situation that he'd ever been in. Inside, the anger reached a point where it turned so hard and cold that his mind became detached, processing his environment like a person watching a movie from the back row of seats. The death of the young girl had done this to him, had shown him a part of himself that he wasn't sure he liked. It was vulgar, the way she'd been used, and it had made him want to kill everything that lived within these loathsome tunnels. Looking back at Terry, he could tell that she felt the same, could see it in her eyes—they spoke volumes from where they glowered from beneath the dirty, makeshift bandage. Even with all her wounds, and her hair tangled in hopeless knots, she was still strikingly beautiful. If nothing else, he would die protecting her, and that, in and of itself, was enough for him to continue.

She was worth the sacrifice.

Moving the light across the monolithic door from top to bottom, she frowned. "Well, Doc, got any bright ideas about how were going to get through this hulking chunk of rock?"

"Yes," he answered, gently pushing her away as he drew the pouch from around his neck. It throbbed in his fingers like a beating heart.

"What are you going to do?"

"Just stand back; I've got an idea. It may not work, but something tells me it will."

She glanced at him with an arched eyebrow but made no reply as she moved back out of the way.

Opening the pouch, he reached in and drew forth the Elder Sign. Its pale form shone in the dimness like a lighthouse beacon, its shimmering whiteness almost blinding them as Terry gasped in surprise.

Holding it out before him, its radiance eclipsing all other illumination, he strode to the door and pressed the talisman firmly against it. With a violent explosion, the mighty rune-inscribed portal imploded, sending chunks of debris flying inward and covering them in a cloud of dust that swirled around them like an opalescent snowstorm.

Williams coughed, then helped Terry up from where she'd fallen as the door disintegrated. In wide-eyed confusion, she stared around, so intent on the bizarre spectacle that she didn't even notice him putting the Elder Sign back in its pouch. She took it all in stride, though, and shook her head to clear it of dust before following him into the shadowy opening.

As she moved through the broken doorway, the shotgun boomed out in the hollow darkness, reverberating off the walls. Her own gun held ready, she rushed through the settling dust and into the chamber beyond.

Williams stood on the shore of a subterranean lake, staring at two more of the disgusting creatures laying in a heap by the stagnant waters. The cavern around them was huge, extending so far back that its dimensions were lost in shadows. There was a small ledge just above and to the left of them that led to the mouth of another tunnel, but it was the lake itself that captured their attention. It was an incredible sight, with iridescent mist playing out across its surface in spiraling patterns that shimmered off the luminescent plant life. Nearby, something blue and yellow floated in the murky liquid. When Williams first spotted the creatures, they'd been using a stick to try and drag the object closer to shore. Viewing it all from the sheltered distance of the archway, he'd fired almost without thinking. The beasts weren't the first creatures that he'd slain this night, and they wouldn't be the last.

Terry crouched next to him, eyeing the corpses with some distaste. "What happened?" she shouted over the vile chanting.

"There were more of those creatures down by the shore. I fired on instinct; I guess I'm getting good at killing. . ."

"Don't say that! Don't you ever say that!" she cried, clutching his arm. "These things are abominations; we've got to destroy the whole nest of them if we can. You weren't killing, you were exterminating! These things, they aren't human! Lord knows what they are, maybe some kind of mutation or something, but they aren't human and they are evil. You saw what they did to that poor girl!"

He nodded, still gazing at the object floating in the brackish water. His detachment no longer allowed for such strong emotions; he'd merely been stating a fact. Shaking loose of her grasp, he stepped forward, hoping to get a better look at what was bobbing on the surface. There was something strange about this body of liquid, something. . .

unclean. The Elder Sign pulsed with increasing urgency from around his neck as he considered the lake with growing unease.

Meanwhile, Terry had scooted forward and was reaching out toward the object. Without thinking, he grabbed her arm, dragging her back.

"What are you doing?" she demanded. "I wanted to get a closer look—"

"When I first saw them," he cut in, pointing to the corpses. "They were trying to pull that thing in with a stick. Let's not be too hasty; it could be dangerous. Besides, I don't trust what I'm seeing. There's something. . . wrong here, something that just doesn't sit well with me. Let's get that stick and try to see if we can drag it closer first."

Soon enough they discovered what had attracted the two beasts; it was another body. This time, the young woman was wearing a blue and gold cheerleading outfit. She floated face down, her blond ponytail trailing out behind her in the murky depths.

As they pulled her closer to shore, he could tell right away that something just wasn't right. She was unexpectedly buoyant, her arms and well-toned legs bobbing on the surface in a highly improbable fashion. Either the lake was a lot shallower than it appeared, or there was something keeping her from sinking down into it.

Hesitating, Williams cursed to himself as he made a snap decision. He had to know what was going on, so he had to take the risk. Leaning forward, he thrust out his hand, grabbing the girl's shoulder, and then flipping her over onto the uneven bank.

"Holy shit!" Terry cried out.

The reasons for the young girl's unaccountable buoyancy were immediately apparent. About two dozen large insectoids had fastened themselves along the front of her torso, their chitinous heads burrowing into her flesh as their segmented, tube-like bodies ran back out under the foul, mist-shrouded water. The things, which were almost as big around as his arm and blue-black in color, clung to the girl's well-tanned flesh with spidery, ill-formed legs. As Williams took in the unpleasant sight, the creatures continued to feed, and he could see the thick, red plasma running sluggishly down the centers of their long, semi-transparent abdomens. It was being taken in slow increments and, as his eyes shot up to the girl's face, he found that one of them was also greedily invading her mouth and burrowing deep into her throat.

They were keeping her alive.

As he came to this startling conclusion, one of the girl's eyes rolled up to stare at him, its deep brown color obscured by a milky sheen. The creature penetrating her mouth was undoubtedly sending oxygen to her lungs and keeping her heart rate steady, but where was all the blood going? He peered out over the body of water with a feeling of bristling fear creeping across his flesh. Then, a movement from beside him caught his attention, and he turned in time to see Terry poking at one of the things with Jarrod's wand. It shuddered as it dug itself in deeper, eliciting a spasm from the helpless girl and a shriek from Terry as its multifaceted eyes clicked open to stare at her with a deep red malevolence.

"Terry, no!" Williams cried, but he was too late—she'd already brought her arm up and then slammed the heavy flashlight down upon the tube-like portion of the creature, severing it from the thorax and spraying them both with hot, sticky ichor.

The reaction from the lake was instantaneous.

The girl was drawn back across the surface as a low, keening moan erupted from the midpoint of the cavern. Then, the very liquid essence of the lake itself began to retract inward, pulling up from the surrounding bedrock and collecting itself in a mountainous expanse near the center. Thousands of eyes began to flicker to life within that gelatinous mound, and at the very apex arose something so heinous that Williams scrambled backward in an unconscious effort to distance himself. All the walls that had kept him aloof were suddenly crumbling, and the voices in his mind cried out in triumph. Or perhaps it was in fear—either way, he knew that they had to get the hell out of there, and fast. Springing to his feet, he grabbed the stunned Terry by the wrist and pulled her toward the edge of the cave.

As they ran for the rocky, lichen-covered wall, the chanting faded under the moaning cry of the entity behind them. The tunnel he'd seen earlier was there, just above them, and he somehow managed to grab Terry around the waist and heave her up onto the small ledge. Risking a glance back, he saw a mountain of roiling tentacles, each tipped by a chittering, multilegged horror, rushing toward him. It was as if the smaller insects were a part of a greater whole, maybe even younger versions of the central being itself, still attached to the parent organism by sickening umbilicals. Or perhaps the limbs were independent entities in-and-of themselves. It made little difference to him now as he frantically battered at the menacing things with the butt end of the rifle. Managing to clear a small space around him, he threw the shotgun up into the tunnel mouth, then scrambled toward the ledge, cutting his hands and knees in his rush to climb to safety.

As he sought purchase on the rocky wall, the teeming arachnids swarmed across his exposed back, their ravenous mouth-parts making gnashing sounds that were far more horrifying than the keening moans arising from the larger beast. His arms and legs were sent into a renewed frenzy of motion and, as he finally reached the top of the ledge, he tried shaking them off, but was quickly engulfed by their droning multitudes.

Gunshots rang out in the darkness, and he was suddenly being hauled from beneath their seething masses. Terry had a hold of his pack and was dragging him into the tunnel, expending rounds while screaming out in fierce defiance. Yet for every multilegged parasite she ruptured, another dozen or so took their place. The mouth of the tunnel was soon choked with a wall of the chittering creatures and Terry's gun was clicking on empty.

Wobbling to his feet, Williams shoved her farther into the corridor, moving them away from an entrance now packed with writhing monstrosities. Wailing and cursing, she continued to pull the trigger on the now useless gun as he tried to shield her from the grasping insectoids as best he could. The echoing chant was all around them now, shuddering throughout the burrow and adding an urgency to the striving bug-like creatures. As he stared into the hundreds of multifaceted eyes, he began to regret having ever touched the floating body.

Curiosity, after all, had killed the cat. . .

He chuckled at the unexpected thought. This was no time for levity, but there it was. He was suddenly overcome by fits of uncontrollable laughter. Oh, this was a real knee-slapper, one for the record books, all right! Caught in the throes of an all consuming hysteria, he was only partially aware when Terry opened his pack and dug around in it. Whatever she was doing, he decided it couldn't possibly be more ridiculous than the scene playing out in front of him. Swaying unevenly, he took a step forward, howling out in insane mirth as he reached toward the pretty glowing lights, the burning, crimson-colored eyes that were now an almost solid wall of rhythmic movement before him.

Grabbing his shoulder, Terry thrust her other arm past him, spraying the chitinous bodies with something from a squeeze can. The sudden smell of kerosene made his eyes water. Then, setting fire to a crumpled bit of rag, she tossed it into the front ranks of the writhing insects. Within seconds, the entire mass of them was engulfed in flames. With an enraged wail from the outer chamber, the burning tentacles were ripped back out of the opening, leaving the air reeking of charred, oily flesh.

"Are you. . . alright?" she asked, collapsing to the floor.

He knew what she was really asking; had he completely lost his mind? He had, temporarily, and it had almost gotten them both killed! But just hearing her question his sanity was like a cold slap in the face. Pulling together the pieces of his fractured mentality, he slumped down next to her and then gave her a brave, half-apologetic smile.

"Yeah, I guess so. Sorry I flaked out on you there. I'm not sure what came over me—I don't even like spiders. . . "

Laughing in unabashed relief, she embraced him. Relaxing into the circle of her arms, he found a strange sort of peace. Even though they were fighting their way through this horrific experience, he was happy with the way they'd come to rely on one another. Not only for support, but for strength in the face of such overwhelming odds. He realized that he'd come to love this brave young woman, and he promised himself right then that he'd tell her of his feelings.

But at that moment the wall suddenly crumbled away, causing tons of soil and rock to rumble outward in a deafening roar that momentarily overpowered the hideous chanting.

Dragging their few possessions along with them, they scrambled back as their refuge deteriorated. There was still enough light from the eerie glow of the phosphorescent vegetation for them to glimpse the cause of the unexpected destruction through a cloud of billowing dust.

Terry whimpered low in her throat, letting the gun slide through her numb fingers as a deep, keening moan washed over them. It was louder, by far, than the chanting, and far more menacing. With hands that seemed to no longer work correctly, Williams fumbled for the shotgun, dragging it along with him as they backed away.

Staring in through the widening gap was a monstrous

entity of unimaginable proportions. Its immense, triangular-shaped head filled the opening as its large, multifaceted eyes lit up the darkness like a cluster of gigantic, red-hot coals. Before they could even react, obscene pink tendrils shot out from between its mandibles, hissing along the floor and uncoiling like a mound of writhing snakes. The sight of it sent them into a flurry of renewed motion as they scrambled to their feet and then ran screaming into the recesses of the pitch-black tunnel.

***

The nebulous, power-infected chamber resonated with the hellish chant, moving in and out of the earthly dimension in a constant state of flux. Just beneath the churning gate, Ezra stood staring up through the vortex and out across the spaces beyond. As the power warped through him, his vision grew more acute, and he was able to discern his faceless god with greater clarity.

Beholding such a creature was an ecstasy never yet felt by him, or his daughter for that matter, and it tore through their shared intellect like a raging storm. Unnoticed, blood began to ooze from his eyes and nose as he stood mesmerized, his stolen body shuddering with internal hemorrhaging as the deity flowed closer through the mists of time and space.

The feeling was. . . orgasmic.

Wavering and groping, the massive, conical-shaped being approached, its magnificent throat tentacle slithering in-and-out of the aperture at its neck. It had no eyes to speak of, nor ears or mouth, but its many-fingered claws reached out from either side of its shifting, irregular body as it lumbered forward on three gargantuan legs. Here was divine retribution incarnate, and pure madness radiated out from it as it made its way inexorably toward the summoning chamber.

Ezra completed the last section of the chant and then the room fell into a silence punctuated only by the entity's flowing discords and the thin whimpering of the unwilling sacrifice. At last the legacy of his forefathers was at hand! This was the moment that he'd been waiting for his entire life.

Raising the shimmering dagger, he plunged it straight into the heaving chest of the struggling captive. With a fountain of blood and a tortured scream, Kelly Miller became one with the void forever.

In adulation, Ezra gazed up at the terror that he'd unleashed, falling to his knees in front of the blood-stained altar. Then, as the monstrous being moved closer across the astral planes, he raised his hands in supplication, blood-red tears draining down his face. But, just as the creature was preparing to come forth from the swirling gateway, the muffled sounds of screaming shattered the silence. Turning, Ezra searched for the source of the disturbance, and was just in time to see the back wall crumbling inward as it deposited two dirt-encrusted people onto the floor.

It was the meddlesome doctor and his assistant.

Thrumming with the changes brought about by the power of his god, an ecstatic grin blossomed across his features. It would be an exquisite pleasure to have a captive audience witnessing his transformation into the most powerful being ever known to man. His rule over the planet would start with these two pitiful souls, and he was not blind to the irony of it all. They had tried to stop him, yet now they would be the first to submit to his will.

Peering back through the hole that they'd managed to dig themselves out of, he could just make out the multi-tendrilled form of the lake denizen groping blindly after them. It could not claim them now in its mindless hunger, for they were under his control and subject to the whims of his newly summoned lord—Nathrotep, the Soul and Messenger of the Outer Gods.

-21-

Terry had lost complete control as they'd thrown themselves against the earthen wall blocking the end of the tunnel. With maddened shrieks, she'd gouged at the obstruction, tearing through it with a ferocity born of terrified desperation. But when the wall had finally given way, they'd fallen head first into the depths of a living nightmare.

"Oh my God, oh my God, oh my God, oh my God. . ." Williams mumbled over and over, the shotgun tumbling from his grasp as he curled into a fetal position.

As she gazed at the crowd of subhuman creatures now surrounding them, Terry moaned in terror, but her eyes were quickly drawn to the flickering radiance coming from the opposite end of the room. There, a great swarm of flying serpents circled a phosphorescent cloud, their elongated snouts giving forth a high-pitched warbling that intermingled with the chilling sounds emanating from the vapor-swirled rent in the air. Something was inside that rotating mist, something that went far beyond what her mind was capable of comprehending. Convulsing into fits of uncontrollable trembling, she stared at the massive arms ending in seven-fingered claws and the obscene throat tentacle slithering from the top of the being's fluctuating, cone-shaped body. Whatever the thing was, it was coming through the vortex, reaching out as its titanic proportions began to fill the room.

With a sudden burst of willpower, she tore her eyes away from it and grabbed Williams by the shirt collar, shaking him like a rag doll. "Barnaby!" she wailed. "Barnaby, God dammit! Get up!"

"I don't think he can hear you anymore, Miss Bradford."

Her head snapped around, eyes searching, and she was shocked when she found the source of that child-like voice.

It was Robin.

But the girl's face was now a horrid mask of bulging veins covering stark white features, the paleness only accentuated by the rivulets of gore streaming from her orifices. The unsettling contrast of the blood against her colorless skin added more depth to the lines of her face than the candle-lit shadows could ever account for. This was the thing from the hypnosis session, the one that Williams had so reluctantly described.

And whatever it was now, it was Robin no longer.

Struggling to draw breath, she quivered in total, mind-numbing fear, knowing that they would surely die here. Williams was unreachable; from where he lay curled into a tight, little ball, all she could hear were the whimpering sounds that a small, frightened child might make. The hellish creatures around her were watching with glowing, bloodshot eyes, their blunt, canine snouts twitching in inhuman hunger but, as she fumbled after the wand, her eyes were drawn yet again to the being in the vortex. It was like something straight out of Dante's Inferno; how could have they ever hoped to defy it?

Her groping hands finally found the end of the tether; it was broken and the wand long gone, probably buried under all the rubble from the collapsing wall. Shuddering and twitching, she sank the rest of the way to the floor, her semi-vacant eyes wandering down to stare at the thing now controlling Robin's body as it continued to speak.

"So, you thought to stop the mighty Nathrotep from taking his place upon the Earth?" it said. "You and your pathetic little lover? All by your insignificant selves? Ha!"

The chamber rang with the sounds of its mockery, accompanied by the powerful droning of the huge entity from where it writhed within the swirling gateway.

"Now I, Ezekial Jedidiah, will lead the world into a new era, and I shall show the race of man pain and suffering like it has never known before! The oceans will rise and the winds shall rip across the continents! The ground will shake, and fires shall blaze across the heavens! This will be the beginning of a new age—the age of chaos! All the minions of my master shall arise, unfettered and unrestrained, spreading out across the land and destroying any who dare to oppose us. Pah! Man is nothing! Just an ill-mannered child race full of weakness and self delusion. The Old Ones were, the Old Ones are, and the Old Ones shall be again! They will walk no more between the spaces, but through them, and they shall wreak their vengeance upon all of mankind! And I. . . I shall become a god!"

Tears rolled down Terry's face as she watched the priest raise his arms in triumph, the flying creatures screeching out their devotion as the massive ancestral being thrust one of its three, pillar-like legs through the dimensional rift. It was coming over into the mortal realm and there was nothing that they could do to stop it.

Just then, a patch of darkness detached itself from the wall, gliding across the intervening space like a wraith out of a madman's fairy tale. As it swept forward, flying across the pitted flagstones, it slammed into Robin's body, shoving her out of the path of the oncoming deity.

Gasping in shock, Ezekial sprang up from where he'd slid to a stop along the rocky floor. "How dare you!" he sputtered.

The figure now standing in the place of the would-be

godling raised its arms to the hood of its pitch-black robe, ignoring the trembling of the air, the angry warbling of the mystical, flying serpents, and the vibrant outcry of the enraged demon.

Lifting the cowl from her face, Carol LePrade glared down at the image of her husband now reborn within the countenance of their only child.

"You may have destroyed all that I hold dear, may have taken the one thing that matters most to me in all the world," she cried, throwing her head back and spreading her arms wide to the cascading energy, "but you will never know the power that you seek! I will now take your place! You will die with the rest and only your ashes will remain, for I, Carol LePrade, will become the new master of all humanity in the age of chaos yet to come. I will be the chosen dispenser of all the Messenger's commands. And. You. Will. Be. Nothing!"

Rumbling out a throaty chuckle, she turned to the writhing monstrosity.

"Oh, Nathrotep, soul of the outer gods, thou who rejoices in the baying of hounds, spilling of blood, and the beating of the eternal drums, accept me! Let me be the one true disciple of all you propose! Accept me!"

"Stop!" Ezekial shouted, causing an almost imperceptible lull in the scattered, intermingled vocalization of the other servitor races. "You will not deny me my rightful place, you filthy whore! I will not lose everything my ancestors strived for, will not fail in my sacred right to become the next high priest! The secrets that my forefathers gained, the hidden knowledge they accumulated, will not be usurped by one such as you!"

Sweeping his arms up, he called out to the Hunting Horrors, sending them forward in an unsteady tide of wavering black flesh, flowing through the air in sinuous unison.

But the towering deity wailed out a string of alien

phrases, thrusting its second leg through the curtain of shimmering magic. It was now standing two-thirds of the way through the swirling gateway, its slithering throat tentacle writhing out across the vaulted ceiling and knocking bits and pieces of stonework down from the shadowy frescoes that resided there.

As his minions scattered, confused by the conflicting commands, Ezekial tried desperately to regain control. However, the mighty Nathrotep spoke again, its thundering voice echoing off the chamber walls, and the Hunting Horrors reformed, their seething masses boiling back toward Ezekial in a cloud of writhing chaos.

With a snarl that was more than half-mad, Ezekial gestured, lashing out with the power at his command and scattering his would-be attackers like leaves upon the wind.

Carol's harsh laughter rang out in peals of derision.

"You can't even control your own minions!" she scoffed, "What good are you to the mighty lord you profess to serve so well?"

Contempt curling at her lips, she stood taller in the shelter of the monstrous being's limbs. The huge, three-toed claws of its feet had scored deep gouges in the floor to either side of her, and its glistening, grayish-pink flesh accentuated her black-robed features in supernatural clarity.

"You are nothing!" she cried. "See how I so easily wield your stolen power. . ."

With that, she gestured to the Hunting Horrors, her hands moving in intricate patterns as she hissed at them in their own language. Instantly they rushed to obey, flying once more in great droves toward the reeling form of Ezekial. With a scornful wave of his hand, he flung them aside yet again.

"You think to defy me, woman? You think that the tiny bit of knowledge you've stolen will sustain you in your treachery? Pah! You are the one who is nothing! I have not even begun to use the power that's been granted me. But I can see now that I'm being tested, that I'm being given the chance to prove that I am worthy of such power. . ."

His hands wove through patterns of immense complexity, and Carol was suddenly slammed backward by an unseen force, turning round and round as she spiraled up into the air. Ezekial crowed out in satisfaction.

"You see?" he bellowed. "You cannot prevail, for I am the master here!"

With a great roar, the mighty god lashed out, capturing the struggling woman and raising her to its slithering tentacle far above. Showers of stone cascaded down from the ceiling as the slimy appendage slathered across the surface of her body, moving to envelop her in its wet embrace. Ezekial howled in rage, realizing that his dark lord was probing her for the latent abilities needed to become the next high priestess in his stead. He could not let that happen.

He would not allow it.

In dumbstruck confusion, Terry watched as the creature coiled its repellent tentacle around the embattled woman, but as the strange altercation played out above her it jolted her back into a frenzy of motion. With a strength born out of desperation, she showered blows down upon Williams where he lay drooling upon the floor. Yet there was still no response from him. They had failed; everything they'd started out to do, all the lives they would have saved, including their own, were now forfeit. The earth would become a wasteland of destruction, and they'd all soon be dead, or far worse.

Rocking back and forth, she keened out in helpless pain, unaware that the pitiless entity was feeding upon her rampaging emotions. Overcome by the soul-shattering realization of all she had lost, her remorse became unbearable, and she began to beat on Williams' prone body with greater force, needing him to get up, to take charge again like he'd done so many times before. But instead he just lay there, wide-eyed and blubbering. Sobbing helplessly, she sank back to the floor with nothing left to give.

Her unsuccessful attempts at waking Williams from his catatonic state went unnoticed by Ezekial. Lifting his hands, the very hands that had once belonged to his only daughter, he uttered the words of a unclean spell, knowing that it was the only chance left for him to reclaim his birthright.

A tremor rent the air and surrounding walls as a dark cloud boiled up from Robin's battered head, something as black and twisted as a cancerous growth. As her limp figure collapsed to the ground, the terrified subhuman creatures fled from the chamber, leaving Terry alone to face the remaining serpent minions and the dark lord that they all served.

-22-

The puppets continued their noisy, sharp-lined play as her fingers smeared blood-soaked patterns on the ground, but Terry had lost interest in dramatic posturings. Williams had stopped his babyish mewling, and she was quite content to be lying there by his side making lazy doodles in the dirt.

She blinked as a tennis shoe-clad foot appeared in front of her.

Curious, but not at all startled, her eyes followed the leg upward until she could see the face of the puppet. He looked angry. This must be the brave hero, she thought, the play once more capturing her attention.

Not taking his eyes from the scene unfolding on the stage, the puppet knelt down and picked up the shotgun from the floor. . .

Wait a minute! Shotgun?

Memories blossomed within her, bits of elusive knowledge falling suddenly into place. It was like being drenched by a splash of icy water—the shock of cold realization followed by a discomforting regret. With torturous clarity, her sense of identity reestablished itself, and she remembered.

She struggled for breath then, like a drowning man desperate for air. It was a long, hard climb out of the pit of delusion that she'd huddled in, but inch by painful inch she began to reclaim what was lost. Not all of it, but enough of an agonizing awareness that it cut her to the bone.

Still, she met the pain head-on and rose above it.

The boy who'd grabbed the shotgun didn't hesitate; a white-hot fury radiated from him as he advanced toward the massive creature. Raising the weapon, he pointed it at the struggling smudge of black so far above them and fired, jacking round after round into the chamber until the muscles of his arms were shuddering from the recoil.

The first shot struck Carol in the shoulder. The second and third shots took off the top of her head, showering the writhing god-thing with blood and sticky debris. The priest had barely enough time to scream before the body he now inhabited was reduced to so much dead weight. His loathsome shadow erupted from the corpse like a cloud of foul smog. It floated free, and Terry could that see it was searching for a new body to posses. As the haze of corrupted darkness turned toward her, she was hit by a momentary wave of paralyzing fear, but then the flying, snake-like creatures converged upon Ezekial's astral form in a flurry of agitated motion. The air became a whirlwind of slick, black coils, serrated wings, and roiling, flashing mists.

Nathrotep howled, dropping the blood-soaked corpse and taking the third and final step over the threshold.

Some of the boy's angry focus dissipated in that moment. Stumbling backward, his face went through a series of uncontrolled spasms as he tried to regain his lost bravado. The throat tentacle, repugnant in its quivering elasticity, snaked forward, scattering the lesser minions as it rippled toward him.

Lurching into him from behind, Terry shoved him out of the way.

"Pick her up, then follow me!" she commanded, the tentacle hissing past them to flail against the far wall before writhing back up into the air.

He looked to where she was pointing, noticing, perhaps for the first time, the pale face of Robin nestled within the folds her tattered robes. Crossing to the altar, he dropped the shotgun and then gathered her into his arms, gazing intently at her bruised and battered face.

Terry shouted a warning and, as his head jerked up, he saw the gigantic, three-legged creature reaching toward him with its massively clawed hands.

As she saw the powerful entity reaching for the boy, Terry briefly lost the ability to form coherent thoughts. But then, driven by some mad compulsion, she bent down and ripped the pouch from around Williams' neck. Drawing forth the pulsating Elder Sign, she cocked her arm back like the pitcher at a baseball game.

"Choke on this, you filthy bastard!" she cried, hurling the glowing talisman toward the shrinking gateway.

The howling of the creature rose to new levels as the shining object arched toward it. In a mighty effort to intercept the spinning relic, its claws shot upward, but the blazing artifact passed right through them.

And vanished into the rift.

Terry didn't pause to witness the outcome of her actions; there just wasn't time. Kneeling, she grabbed Williams under the arms and began dragging him toward the tunnel she'd seen Carol entering through earlier.

That's when an explosion of rhythmic forces nearly knocked her from her feet. Squinting her eyes against the intense glare, she quelled her rising panic and motioned for the boy to hurry. But he was gazing down at Robin again, seemingly lost in thought. Struggling with Williams and cursing under her breath, Terry yelled, "Move it!"

Flinching like a startled dog, he glanced up and then ran for the tunnel opening. She only looked back once on that hellish place, but the scars of that moment would be forever imprinted upon her fragile mind. Nathrotep flailed the air with its fluidic appendages, raging against the bonds of fiery, white light that had wrapped it from head to toe. Of Ezekial there was no sign—just the flying creatures swirling in angry confusion and then slowly fading into the nothingness of the between. As the ceiling began to crumble and the floor cracked open, she saw the beginnings of an end to that terrible chamber, an ending that would span worlds and send aftershocks of unequaled force surging all throughout the cosmos.

Then, they were fleeing for their lives.

***

Mark ducked into the tunnel and, as he felt Robin stir in his arms, he realized that she'd somehow become very important to him. He didn't know why, only that he now had feelings for her that defied all reason. A memory surfaced; a flash of pale moonlight, an open window, the press of warm lips against his own. Shaking his head in bewilderment, he moved deeper into the gloomy passageway, striving to keep survival utmost in his thoughts. Not only for Robin and himself, but for the strange woman, whoever she was, that had saved them all. Glancing back, he could see her pulling the afflicted man along the uneven, rubble-strewn floor, but it was slowing her down.

Slowing them both down.

Anger surged anew, blotting out all other emotion except brutal rationality.

"Leave him," he shouted. "He's just dead weight!"

The look that she turned on him was one of such pain and violence that his boiling rage was all but eclipsed by it. Raising her right hand, she clenched and unclenched her index finger, almost as if she were pointing something at him, something that she no longer possessed.

Uncertain of what to do, he stood his ground, glaring

back at her.

As she realized what she was doing, she shook herself a little, some of the fire going out of her eyes to be replaced by an edge of sorrow so deep that he gasped.

"We. . . we can't just leave him!" She gestured with trembling hands, eyes sheathed in a glistening wetness. "He's still alive! I. . . I just can't!"

Leaning forward, he held Robin out to her. "It's gotta be one or the other; we can't carry them both and still make it —we don't even know where this tunnel leads! Make up your goddamn mind! In case you hadn't noticed, this whole shitshow is about to become. . . become. . ." he faltered, then in a softer tone, just below the high-pitched shrieking of the beast, "whatever the fuck this place is turning into back there. . ."

Terry stared at him, then glanced back at the tunnel entrance, the indirect light flashing across the tears spilling down her cheeks. Her agony all but squeezed the life from her, yet there could be no other solution. There just wasn't time.

Leaning down with a barely suppressed sob, she kissed Williams on the cheek. "I love you, you know," she whispered. Then, they were running down the tunnel and away from the horrors that lay beneath that ancient graveyard, the site that had inspired so much madness in them all.

Unseen by anyone left alive in that accursed place were the tracks of a single tear as it made its way down the pale, motionless face of Doctor Barnaby Williams.

-23-

The next few minutes were a blur as Mark ran through the dimly lit corridors which spiraled out from the central chamber and then angled upward to run beneath the graves of the old graveyard itself. While they made their way through this maze of interlocking tunnels, there were creatures coming out of the semi-darkness that were a nightmare to behold, but the beasts took no notice of them, seeming to be far more intent upon running for their own lives. Their high-pitched, canine cries resounded throughout the warren as Mark forged ahead, often shoving through groups of the fleeing creatures as they progressed down the eerily glowing passageways.

From behind them came the incessant throb of malevolent energy as they continued, always moving, never stopping in their headlong flight from that cavern where he'd first awoken. Fear was now their greatest motivator—fear of being overwhelmed by the creatures around them, of being overcome by the powers erupting behind them, or of simply being buried alive beneath the partially collapsing burrows. It was all this and more which drove him onward, never slowing, never looking back, until they reached a small chamber at the very end of the last, shadowy tunnel.

A dead end.

"My God," the woman moaned, "w-what do we do

now?"

Glancing around, Mark nodded at the broken casket that occupied the center of the small area. "Climb up—we'll have to dig ourselves out."

Without hesitation, she jumped on top of the wooden box and began gouging into the moist earthen ceiling with both hands.

"Dig faster!" Mark shouted, going down on one knee as he balanced Robin across his other leg.

"Shut the hell up!" she snapped back at him, her nails breaking as she dug into the more firmly packed dirt above the wet soil. "I'm doing the best that I can!"

"Well, it ain't good enough! Get a move on or we'll all be toast!"

"You think this is easy?" she shrilled. "Why don't you give me the girl, and you get up here and dig?" She paused then, her eyes going wild as she struggled to catch her breath. "Oh my God. . ." she moaned, "we're going to die down here, aren't we?"

The silence was ominous as her last words echoed strangely in the confines of the small space.

Peering back down the now unnaturally quiet tunnel, they were struck by a sense of foreboding so profound that it compelled them into immediate action.

"Dig, dammit, dig!" Mark screamed.

The woman began clawing at the ceiling with renewed energy, her sobbing breaths echoing loudly in the air around them. As she scrabbled at the crumbling soil, the niche began to vibrate with a feeling of uncleanliness, a resonance of total repugnance that they could feel right down to their bones. Throwing Robin across one shoulder, Mark stood and then leapt onto the casket himself, reaching up to tear at chunks of earth and rock with his free hand.

They were still digging frantically when the thundering over-spill of the collapsing gate's unclaimed power overtook them, the waves of its putrescence boiling outward like a ceaseless, oncoming tide. Their lingering, raw-throated cries were quickly swallowed up by the pulsating harmonics, the tainted energy hammering into them as they continued to gouge their way through the ceiling of the collapsing grave.

Mark was fighting against the clods of dirt and grass showering down all around them when the woman was suddenly yanked upward, disappearing through the loosened soil. Shuddering with uncontrollable fear, he wrapped his arms tightly around Robin, howling in terror as the roughened hands of some unknown creature thrust themselves down to grasp at his neck and shoulders. He resisted, but more than one set of hands had a hold of him then, and they pulled him into the stormy night of the world above. Only his convulsive grip on Robin's unresponsive form kept him from dropping her as they both emerged from the ground and then sprawled across the dampened grass. Spitting out mouthfuls of filth, he glanced fearfully around. Of the creatures, there was no sign, but he found that there was a sodden lump of a man kneeling in the windswept darkness. The strange woman was crouching next to him, both of them covered in mud up to their shoulders.

"I'm sorry," the man was saying, "I am so sorry—"

"It's not your fault," the women interjected in a quavering voice, "I'm the one who f-failed, the one who l-left him behind. . ."

"Now you just hush that, young lady!" the man replied. "It were a damn fool's errand that I let you folks go on in the first place, and a selfish one at that! I thought you might be the ones to finally avenge my sweet Barbara's murder. But, by the time I know'd you'd bitten off more than you could chew, there was nothing I could do. I had to hang round out here, hoping you'd make it out alright, hoping I could do something more iffen you did. It were all I could do with what little power I have just to locate your position under these here graves. I should of helped you more from the get-go, been prepared to take more of a risk, but, like I said afore, I just ain't strong enough. I coulda never faced up to the sort of things that was going on down in them tunnels. Whatever's happened to you, the loss of your friend. . . well, that's all because of me, because I'm such a damn coward. . ."

"Jarrod!" the women cried, "it wasn't your fault! You gave us what we needed to survive, helped us to understand what was going on in the first place. Without you, we'd all be dead! Besides, I'm the one who left him. I-I left him to die!"

It was more than Mark could take. He didn't know who the fat man was, and he really didn't care—all this crying and carrying on was for pussies. Struggling to his knees, he grabbed Robin under the arms and then dragged her over to a fallen grave marker. Flopping down beside her, he fought to catch his breath as he gazed up at the ominously churning clouds. They were unlike any clouds that he'd ever seen before.

Pulling his eyes away from the disturbing maelstrom going on above him, he glanced back toward the shuddering, light-filled manor instead. It was now heaving with sullen power. Thick, coiling tendrils of malignant force were flowing outward from it in never-ending waves, and, within those waves, a wind was gathering. As he watched, debris began to spiral upward from the center of the house, its rotted walls jettisoning materials in heavy streams of disintegrating particles.

When the outer edges of this energy-infused whirlwind began to sweep over him, he glimpsed a vortex appearing in the turbulent sky above the dwelling. Reaching down through a hole in the middle of those dark, swirling clouds was a creature of unimaginable proportions, a being so interwoven with the strands of evil that its very nature was a tapestry of perpetual nightmare. With a concentrated effort, he managed to wrest his eyes away from it and was shocked to then witness Jarrod's hair turning bone-white as the man continued to gaze up at the hellish thing. Peering back at the house through tear-blurred vision, Mark saw the writhing, tentacled monstrosity from the underground chamber rising up from the bowels of the earth. It was drawn into the rift by the greater entity, and with a final rumble of thunder and a burst of electrified air, the vortex collapsed, leaving him feeling weak and sickened inside.

Falling forward onto her hands, the woman let the nausea run its course, spewing out a thin stream of bile as the fat man, his eyes now wide and empty, simply toppled to the ground. Mark was left struggling alone against the terrible events they'd just experienced, trying desperately to shake the visions of it from his fractured mind.

Above him, the light of dawn was creeping across the rapidly clearing sky, painting the graveyard in reddish colors as he searched for a distraction, something, anything, to take his thoughts away from the maddening events of the last few hours. Scanning past the heaving woman and the vacant-eyed man, they came to rest on Robin's battered, upturned face. With a trembling hand, he reached out and brushed aside a lock of her tangled hair. Her features, although bloody and badly bruised, had an ethereal quality, almost like that of a fallen angel. There was just something about her, something that drew him like a moth to a flame.

Enraptured, he took her hand, struggled to come to grips with the confusing emotions that he was now experiencing, but when her eyes fluttered open to gaze up at him, he let it fall back from his lax grasp in acute embarrassment. As he watched, a tremulous smile spread across her bloodied lips, and he was suddenly hit by a rush of such heartfelt longing that it almost felt like a betrayal. Kelly was dead! How could he already be feeling this way about her best friend? But as her smile widened, exposing dull, white teeth in a curious grin, his traitorous spirit practically soared in response.

"Robin?" he ventured, "Robin, it's me, Mark. You know; Mark Cook, from school? Are you. . . okay?"

Her response drove him to his feet and sent him stumbling backward. As he struck his hip on another upright slab, he spun around and then slammed into a headstone that the other woman was leaning against. Fighting for control, he stared back at Robin in outright shock.

She was laughing!

Howling, really. A great series of pealing cackles that were frighteningly inhuman. Her ululating cries split the morning air and, as he stood mesmerized by her twitching features, she sat up and began rocking back and forth on the cold, weather-beaten stone, her bloodshot eyes wide yet unseeing. Not knowing what else to do, he turned, desperate for guidance from the older woman.

The woman, however, was no longer kneeling; she'd lurched up from the ground and was now standing right next to him, her face only inches from his own. Grabbing him by the shoulders, she began screaming incoherently, her blood-curdling cries alternating with Robin's howls of deranged laughter as her fingers dug painfully into his flesh. With a wrench, he tore himself from out of her grasp, falling to the ground with his mouth hanging open in complete astonishment.

They were both stark-raving mad!

Climbing back to his feet, he decided that he was about done with all this weird bullshit. Edging away from the stricken pair, he noticed for the first time the sounds of sirens in the crisp morning air. The police would be there soon, maybe even the fire department—they would probably blame this whole fucked-up mess on him!

Staring at the shrieking woman, the fallen, vacant-eyed man, and the cackling, maddened thing that had somehow become his heart's fondest desire, he shook his head in mute denial. Then he turned from them and fled across the field of unkempt graves.

He ran for miles that morning, not even noticing the eyes that were following his progress from the remaining burrows of that hellish place, running until he had no strength left, and then running some more. Through the surrounding neighborhoods he fled, away from the sirens and the screaming laughter, away from the ancient graveyard, and far away from everything that he had ever known.

Something inside his mind told him how it would be then, explained to him what he now needed to do.

He would leave this sacred place and then wait for the 'call'. When it came, he would know it, and he would be ready to answer. Running from the dawn and all it revealed, Mark Cook headed for the outskirts of town, knowing that, someday, when the stars were right, he would return.

Someday.

About the Author

William H. Nelson is the author of **Nathrotep** (Blysster Press 2018). He grew up in Anchorage, Alaska, where he attended college at UAA. During his time there, he was a regular contributor to several publications, including, **The Radical** (Radical Publications, 1992-94), **The Auroran** (Denali Publications 1993-96), and **Rainsongs** (Denali Publications 1995-96).

After moving to the Seattle area in 1998, he eventually met the love of his life, Lisa, and now lives with her and their cat, Dipso, (named from the Greek word meaning 'thirsty'). William continues to write every day, and in his spare time he enjoys reading voraciously, playing the drums like a berserk spider monkey, creating award-winning costumes and props for local conventions, watching movies with a passion bordering on obsession, and playing selections from his truly ginormous collection of epic fantasy board games.

Connect with William on Facebook!
www.facebook.com/williamhnelsonbooks

CPSIA information can be obtained
at www.ICGtesting.com
Printed in the USA
FSHW02n1105230618
49475FS